DEVIL UNDER THE SKIN

The Merrymakers concert party was near the end of the road. Howard Layton, player-manager of the troupe, sensed he was fighting a losing battle against the competition of cinema and radio, and his audiences in the small towns and villages of East Anglia were rapidly shrinking. But it was the murder of the young star of the show that proved hardest to bear. For Debbie was his daughter and he and his wife Gloria had had ambitious plans for her career on the stage. Why would anyone want to kill her?

DEVIL UNDER THE SKIN

DEVIL UNDER THE SKIN

by
James Pattinson

Dales Large Print Books
Long Preston, North Yorkshire,
England.

British Library Cataloguing in Publication Data.

Pattinson, James
   Devil under the skin.

A catalogue record for this book is
available from the British Library

ISBN 1-85389-577-6 pbk

First published in Great Britain by Robert Hale, 1991

Published in Large Print October, 1995 by arrangement with
Robert Hale.

Dales Large Print is an imprint of
Library Magna Books Ltd.
Printed and bound in Great Britain by
T.J. Press (Padstow) Ltd., Cornwall, PL28 8RW.

Contents

1 Death in a Barn

The barn was one of a sort common enough in East Anglia; it was made of clay lump, a typical building material of the region in past times, tarred black on the outside and roofed with pantiles. It stood in isolation at the edge of a field of mangolds, partly screened from the road by a neglected and overgrown thorn-hedge. A rotting five-barred gate in the hedge gave access to the building, which was also in a dilapidated condition, some of the clay having been eroded by rain-water and a few of the tiles lifted off by the wind and never replaced.

None of this decay, however, was visible when the boy approached it. The time was nearing seven o'clock on an October evening and the only light was coming from a portion of moon which appeared now and then through breaks in the clouds. This light, such as it was, revealed the barn only as a dark mass which to the boy's heightened imagination seemed to have about it an aura of menace. He was seventeen years old and was in a state of high nervous tension, his heart thumping wildly.

He carried a torch in his right hand, but he did not switch it on until he had reached the door of the barn and groped his way inside. Even then he hesitated for a while, standing with his back to the rickety door and peering into the gloom.

He spoke softly, just one word, a girl's name: 'Debbie!' Then listened, holding his breath.

There was no reply. He spoke again, rather more loudly. 'Debbie! Answer me, please. Oh, do please answer, Debbie.'

Only then, when there was still no response to his plea, did he switch on the torch. The beam of light found her at once, as though she had attracted it by some kind of magnetic force. She was lying on a pile of old hay, not moving, as still as death.

'Oh, God!' His voice was like a sob catching in his throat, a cry of anguish and despair. 'Oh, God, don't let it be. Dear God, don't let it be.'

But he knew that the prayer was useless, knew that it was indeed death which was the cause of this awful stillness, this terrible silence. He was appalled by the dreadful irreversible nature of what had happened. What had been done could not be undone, now or ever.

'Debbie! Debbie!'

He could see the handle of the knife protruding from her chest like some obscene growth. He could see the blood; such a lot of blood, staining everything. He had never in all his life seen so much blood.

He approached her slowly, tentatively. He knew that she was dead, had to be; it was impossible that there could be any life remaining in her, lying so still, so utterly still. Yet he felt the need to make absolutely sure nevertheless. It was necessary. He had to touch her, though he shrank from doing so, repelled by the blood and the sight of the knife plunged into her breast.

Her eyes were open, and when he drew closer it seemed to him that she was staring at him, following his every movement with a curious intentness. He sensed the accusation in this gaze, and it troubled him more than the blood.

'Don't look at me like that,' he muttered.

There were tears in his own eyes and his vision was blurred. The torch shook in his hand and the shadows moved around him like a crowd of phantoms. He wanted to turn and run away, to leave that frightful scene, to flee from the barn and its shadows and keep on running.

But he forced himself to stoop and touch the girl's face. There was still some warmth and softness in the cheeks, but he was not deceived; this was no more than the last fading imprint of a life that had already departed. The girl was dead, and soon the warmth and the softness would be gone also, giving place to the chill and stiffness of a corpse.

He drew his hand away, shuddering. Oh, God! he thought. How could this have happened? How could it? He would never have believed it possible. It was worse than the worst of nightmares, and from this there would be no blessed awakening.

He turned away and stumbled towards the door. He stepped out into the night and fled from the barn, scarcely aware of where he was going, knowing only that he had to get away from that horrible place.

2 Advance Notice

There was a printed poster stuck up in the window of Mr Alfred Ringer's grocery shop, announcing the imminent arrival in the village of The Merrymakers concert party. The stay would be for one week only, during which period the troupe would be performing nightly at the Clover Hall, with matinées on the Thursday and Saturday.

The Merrymakers paid a regular visit to Braddlesham in the autumn, squeezing it in between somewhat longer runs at the neighbouring market towns of Heyworth and Sawborough. Braddlesham, known locally as Brasham, was too small a place to be a very profitable venue for the concert party, but as Mr Howard Layton, manager of the troupe, remarked, it filled a gap in the circuit and if takings covered expenses he was reasonably satisfied.

These were difficult times in the world of live entertainment, what with the competition of the cinema and the wireless to contend with. Too many people preferred to stay in the comfort of their own homes listening to Gillie Potter and Mabel Constanduros or the Palm Court Orchestra rather than pay for a hard wooden seat in a draughty hall where flesh-and-blood entertainers went through their routines on a rickety stage. It was a pity, but there it was; and in his more gloomy moments Mr Layton wondered just how much longer it would be before troupes like The Merrymakers were finished, the entertainers themselves thrown out of work and forced to look for other jobs at a time when unemployment was at an unprecedented level and dole queues were lengthening by the day.

Howard Layton had been in the business for more years than he cared to remember. He had been born into it; his father and mother being members of a company of barnstormers who travelled from place to place performing melodramas such as 'Maria Marten', 'Sweeney Todd' and 'Ten Nights in a Bar-room.' He himself had appeared in small parts at a very early age and had learnt to act by imitating the extravagant gestures and facial expressions of some of the hammiest practisers of

14

the Thespian art. With The Merrymakers he performed dramatic monologues and took part in some of the short sketches which lent variety to the song and dance routines.

At the age of sixty Howard Layton, a tall, thin, stooping man with a leonine mane of greying hair and a cadaverous appearance, had a feeling of disillusionment. There had been a time long ago when he had had great hopes of achieving something worthwhile in the profession; but those hopes had faded. He was too old now to deceive himself with the belief that he would ever do anything better than scrape a precarious living from one year to the next; this was the modest limit of his ambition for himself, and he knew that even this might not be possible if things continued on their downward course.

If it had not been for Debbie, Layton thought, he would have been sorely tempted to throw his hand in, to try something else, though he could not have said what, seeing that he had no qualifications for any other kind of job and that unskilled men of his age were hardly the sort employers were looking for. But for Debbie's sake he would not

15

give up yet, not until he had guided her to the kind of success which had always eluded him. For if there was one thing he really believed in, indeed had to believe in if life were to mean anything at all, it was that she was going to reach the top.

And Gloria believed it too.

Gloria Layton was a good ten years younger than her husband, and they had come together when both were performing with a troupe of pierrots at a south-coast seaside resort. Gloria had been a dancer then, young and lissom, with dark hair and wide-set eyes and a little turned-up nose; a real charmer. She had put on a good deal of weight since then and there was a lot of grey in her hair, but Layton had no need to search his memory for a picture of what she had been like in those days; he simply had to look at Debbie.

Deborah Layton was just eighteen years old, and to Layton's way of thinking was an exact replica of what her mother had been when he had first set eyes on her. Gloria did not entirely agree; there were differences, perhaps more apparent to her than to Howard; but there could be no doubt that Debbie was an attractive girl.

One of those differences that her mother noticed had nothing to do with her physical appearance but was a matter of temperament. Gloria had always been of a placid disposition, accepting things as they came and perfectly well aware of the limitations of her own abilities as an artiste. But Debbie was not like that; she was more vivacious, wanted more out of life and meant to have it, always reaching for something just beyond her grasp. She had ambitions; for her The Merrymakers represented no more than a ladder by which she would mount to higher ground where she would make a name for herself, a name that really meant something. One day...

Howard and Gloria shared these ambitions; on this point they were in complete agreement: Debbie was going to make it to the big time.

Layton would cite Jessie Matthews as an example. 'She got to the top, so why not Deb?'

Indeed it seemed far from being beyond the bounds of possibility. The fact was that young Miss Layton bore more than a passing resemblance to the delightful Miss Matthews; people remarked upon it. She could dance, she could act, and though her singing voice would never have filled the Albert Hall or Covent Garden Opera House with discerning music-lovers, it was pleasing enough and perfectly adequate for putting across a popular song of the kind Mr Ivor Novello was so adept at writing.

Howard Layton was convinced that all she needed was the chance to show what she could do in more exalted company than The Merrymakers concert party. He regretted that she had to perform so far away from the hub of the theatrical world; his dream was that one of the powerful London impresarios would see her and recognize her talent and put her in a West End show; but unfortunately impresarios did not make a habit of seeking promising material in travelling companies like The Merrymakers; they had more profitable ways of occupying their time.

Still, some day, somehow... In the end the dream had to come true; it had to. Meanwhile, he did what he could to bring that day forward: he wrote letters, he enclosed photographs, notices cut from the pages of provincial newspapers, anything to whip up a bit of interest; and all to no effect. Perhaps, he thought, a better method would be to get lodgings for

Debbie in London so that she could try to get auditions for shows. Even if she only made it to the chorus line it would be a start; there she would be under the eyes of people who mattered and it would surely not be long before she was picked out from the crowd.

Debbie herself was in favour of this plan, but there were snags. Both Howard and Gloria hesitated to expose their daughter to the perils of being on her own in London; there was no telling what might happen to her; it was not a safe place for a young girl. It would have been different if they had been able to keep an eye on her, but that was out of the question; there was the necessity of earning a living.

Expense, of course, was another consideration; finances were on a knife-edge as it was, and the added cost of maintaining Debbie in London while she looked round for employment would have been an extra burden quite impossible to be borne. There would, too, have been the need for a replacement in the troupe, and where could one find someone to take the place of such a gem? Time and again Howard and Gloria Layton had talked the matter over and the discussion had always ended in sighs of resignation. For the present at least nothing could be done. Debbie would have to remain with The Merrymakers.

Mr Ringer always experienced a slight thrill when Mr Howard Layton walked into his shop with the poster to put in his window. Layton was a being from a different kind of world; the world of grease-paint and footlights and make-believe; a world inhabited by people who were somehow larger than life, romantic, mysterious creatures who had no truck with ordinary mundane jobs like selling pounds of sugar and tins of baking-powder; a world conjured up by two magical words: the stage.

For Mr Ringer it mattered nothing that Howard Layton, driving down from Heyworth with the advance Merrymakers publicity in his bull-nosed Morris Cowley tourer, was somewhere near the bottom of the heap in the theatrical world; that his long overcoat with the astrakhan collar was a trifle threadbare and frayed at the cuffs; that his wide-brimmed black felt hat had seen better days and that his shoes were somewhat down-at-heel. The general impression of seediness about Layton did not even register with Ringer; to him the manager was by way of being a god stepping down from the heights of Mount Olympus to mingle with ordinary human beings. And despite the seediness, Layton had a certain air of superiority about him; his walk was a kind of act in itself; he stepped into the grocer's shop as though making a stage entrance and his voice had a rich fruitiness which gave the lie to any hints of stringency in his outward appearance.

'Ah, Mr Ringer! So we meet again! I trust I find you in rude health?'

'Pretty well, Mr Layton, pretty well. Can't complain.'

'And your good lady?'

'She's well, too.'

'I am gratified to hear it.'

Layton passed the poster across the counter to Ringer, who was a rather plump little man with thinning mousey hair and gold-rimmed glasses. He was wearing a white apron and a black alpaca jacket, shiny at the elbows. The shop had a mingled odour of dried fruit, coffee, tea, cheese, spices and various other commodities. There were biscuits in square tins waiting to be weighed out, bacon hanging from hooks and hessian bags of dried peas and beans.

Layton felt in his pocket and produced two complimentary tickets for the opening performance. These he handed to Mr Ringer, who accepted them with thanks.

'It'll be a real treat for me and the wife. I don't need to ask if it's good this year; it always is.'

'Best ever,' Layton said. 'New songs, new dances, new sketches. Top-notch. Tell your customers.'

'I will. What I always say is, the cinema's all very well in its way but it's not like the real thing, is it? Just pictures, not flesh and blood.'

'True,' Layton said. 'Very true. Well, I must be getting along. More calls to make. No rest for the wicked and precious little for the virtuous either, eh?'

He made his exit with a flourish and went on his way, distributing play-bills and complimentary tickets here and there with a kind of theatrical largesse, making the grand gesture everywhere he went and finishing at the Queen's Head, where he took lunch and reserved accommodation for the members of The Merrymakers troupe for the following week. There were plenty of rooms at the Queen's Head; it was a one-time coaching inn and in the good old days had done a brisk business providing meals and beds for weary travellers. There was still ample stabling at the rear of the inn, but the coaches no longer came and nowadays cars were more likely to be seen in the yard than horses and carts, though some farmers still favoured this earlier form of transport. There was, however, no great demand for the beds and the landlord was pleased to have Mr Layton's custom.

'It's people like you, sir, as bring a bit of life into the village. Ain't much going on most of the time; not in the entertainment line, that is. There's the whist-drives and the dances of course, but they're not quite the same thing, are they?'

'No,' Layton said, 'I wouldn't suppose they were.'

The innkeeper, whose name was Simmonds, was a beery-looking man with an ample stomach and brawny arms. He had been a sergeant in the infantry in the Great War and still sported a waxed moustache twisted into sharp spikes on each side of his upper lip. Layton knew that if you gave him half a chance he would launch into interminable stories of his time in France, where, according to his own account, he had done some pretty heroic deeds. Layton had been caught once or twice and now took good care to give Simmonds no excuse for starting on any subject of a military nature.

It was Mrs Simmonds who, with the help of a sixteen-year-old girl, looked after the guests. She was a lean, sharp-featured woman, with no inclination whatever to indulge in small-talk. She was a human dynamo, always on the go. People said that without her Simmonds would have been lost. Layton was inclined to believe it; mentally, he would have said, Ada Simmonds was two steps ahead of her husband, and maybe more. One thing was certain; she made a first-class job of the catering. She had been cook in a large country house before Simmonds came along and charmed her into marriage with the aid of his waxed moustache and his military bearing, and it was Layton's opinion that he had had the best of the bargain.

Having taken his time over lunch and smoked a Gold Flake cigarette, Howard Layton took the Morris Cowley from the inn-yard where he had left it and drove back to Heyworth to rejoin his troupe.

There he was to find trouble awaiting him.

3 Boy and Girl

Mr and Mrs Ringer had two children, a boy aged seventeen and a girl of fourteen. In a physical way the girl, Angela, was inclined to take after her father, which was unfortunate for her, seeing that Ellen Ringer was slim and still attractive even though she was nearing forty. Angela was dumpy, heavy-featured and stringy-haired. She was painfully aware of her lack of feminine charm and it did nothing to sweeten her temper.

It was the son, Mark, who seemed to have inherited his mother's good looks; he was a handsome fair-haired boy, well-built and athletic, on whom girls and even women often cast languishing glances. His mother would have liked him to become a teacher; she herself had taught in an elementary school before marrying Alfred

Ringer and she had a great respect for education.

For Mark, however, the teaching profession held no attraction whatever. He had left Heyworth Grammar School at the age of sixteen with a creditable Cambridge Schools Certificate but no other qualifications for a successful career and he really had little idea of what he wanted to do. At present he was studying by correspondence course for a Civil Service examination, having been beguiled by an advertisement in a Sunday newspaper which stated: 'NO PASS, NO FEE!' Both his parents had doubts about the wisdom of this project. Mr Ringer thought there had to be a catch somewhere and Mrs Ringer felt that you could not study successfully at home; you needed to go to college or something like that. But Mark persuaded them to let him have a go at it.

'What have we got to lose?'

Mr Ringer thought he could lose the ten guineas he would be expected to lay out on the course; he put no faith in that 'No pass, no fee' promise. But in the end he stumped up and Mark was given the use of a small back room on the first floor as a study. Soon after his enrolment a parcel of text books arrived, together with a typewritten outline of the course of study on which he was embarking. Now he was in correspondence with a tutor in London whom he had never seen and whose name he did not even know, who marked the completed test papers he sent in and pointed the way to the next stage of his education.

Mark himself was none too optimistic regarding his prospects; the Civil Service examination was a competitive one and he knew that of the hundreds of young people who entered for it only a relative handful were taken on. There were so many youngsters looking for work these days and not enough jobs to go round. For him the correspondence course was really a means of postponing the evil day when he would be forced to go out into the world and search for employment. And then if he failed to find anything else to do he knew that he would have to help in the shop.

He did not want to help in the shop. He had no desire to follow in his father's footsteps; the very idea of being a shopkeeper was anathema to him. At the grammar school he had always been ashamed of the fact that his father was a grocer and would have kept it a secret if that had been possible; it seemed such a low-class occupation. He wished that he could have said that his father was a solicitor or an estate agent or a farmer even; almost anything but a grocer. He knew this was a snobbish attitude to take, but it made no difference; he could not alter the way he felt.

The Ringers had tea soon after six o'clock because that was when the shop closed. They took their meals in a room at the back which was next to the kitchen. The house, of which the shop was a part, was a rambling old building dating back to Georgian times; it had had various alterations and additions in the course of the years and there were rooms in all sorts of odd corners and on different levels connected by narrow passageways and creaking stairs. At the top of the house were attics with dormer windows jutting out of the steep tiled roof which was inclined to leak when there were heavy rainstorms, and zinc baths and buckets were placed in strategic positions to catch the water that came through. The attics were reputed to be haunted, but none of the Ringers had ever seen a ghost.

Tea was a substantial meal and they all ate with good appetite. Mr Ringer, seated at one end of the well-laden table on a Windsor chair, brought up the subject of the forthcoming visit of The Merrymakers to the village.

'Had Mr Layton in the shop today. The actor-manager, you know.'

Angela gave a sniff. 'Actor-manager! Is that what he calls himself? Some actor!'

'Now, now, my girl! There's no need to be so contemptuous. He's a real old trouper, is Mr Layton.' Mr Ringer brought out the word with some relish; it showed he was familiar with the jargon of the stage. 'One of the best.'

Angela was not impressed. She gave another sniff. 'If he's one of the best what's he doing with a measly little company appearing in places like Braddlesham? I mean to say, it's not really theatre at all, is it?'

'Well, of course it's not the West End,' Ringer admitted, 'but the West End isn't everything. There is such a thing as provincial theatre.'

'Yes, but Braddlesham isn't even that. If it's any theatre at all it's parish hall theatre. Good enough for unsophisticated audiences, I suppose, but that's about all.'

Mr Ringer gave an indulgent smile. 'And you are sophisticated? Is that it?'

'I'm not saying I am, but I'm sure I've got better taste than most people round here. We're studying *The Wild Duck* at school. That's really something.'

'You're studying what?' Ringer sounded bemused.

'*The Wild Duck*. It's a play by Ibsen, the Norwegian dramatist. But I don't suppose you've even heard of him.'

'Now don't be sarcastic, Angela.' Mrs Ringer spoke sharply. 'You should think yourself lucky your father is seeing to it that you get a better education than he was able to have.'

Angela looked sulky. 'Well—'

Ringer, not altogether relishing this defence of himself on the part of his wife, said: 'Let's not go into that.' He turned to his daughter. 'So are we to take it that you won't be going to see The Merrymakers next week?'

She wriggled her shoulders. 'Oh, I don't know. If there's nothing better to do I might go along.'

'You don't think it would be too unsophisticated for you?' Mr Ringer asked chaffingly.

She gave another wriggle of the shoulders but said nothing.

'How about you, Mark? You'll go?'

'Oh, I dare say.' Mark was studiously offhand, striving to give the impression that he cared little one way or the other; whereas the truth of the matter was that the imminent arrival of the concert party in the village had thrown him into a fever of expectation. 'It'll make a change, I suppose.'

'Well,' Ringer said, 'I can see there's a lot of enthusiasm in the younger members of this family. I'm sure Mr Layton would be very gratified if he knew how eagerly you two are looking forward to his visit.' He spoke lightly, but he was rather put out nevertheless. He was disappointed by their attitude; it seemed to belittle Mr Howard Layton and ridicule his own admiration for the man. For them it was obviously no big thing to shake the hand of an actor-manager, or at least not one who included in his circuit such places as Braddlesham. He sighed faintly. That was the younger generation for you.

He had no suspicion that the outward show of indifference on the part of his son was merely a smoke-screen put up in order to disguise his true feelings from the other three. They would have been astonished if Mark had told them just how deeply he was involved with The Merrymakers concert party, or at least with one particular member of that troupe. He could imagine the concern, even consternation, it would have aroused in his father and mother if they had known, though Angela would probably have received the information with a hoot of derision. For there was no love lost between the brother and sister.

So no one must know about his relationship with Debbie; not yet; perhaps not for years. It was all so difficult and yet so exciting. Even Mr and Mrs Layton were ignorant of what had taken place almost under their very noses; they had been occupied with other matters. And Debbie had been insistent that her parents should be told nothing.

'This is our secret, Mark,' she had said. 'People would never understand.'

He was not so sure she was right about that; it should have been easy enough to understand: a boy and a girl falling in love with each other; it was the most natural thing in the world, and the oldest. But he did not argue with her; they were agreed on the vital point: it had to be kept a secret.

'For the present. But some day of course it will have to come out. Some day we'll tell the world.'

'Oh,' she had said, 'some day anything may happen. It's a long way off.'

He could see the truth in that. Looking to the future he could not foresee a time when he would be in a position to marry. Unless he landed that Civil Service post. But to achieve that he would have to come near the top in the competitive examination, and when he was being perfectly honest with himself he had no great confidence in his ability to do anything of the kind. There were so many others working away like beavers to attain the same object, and why should he imagine he was brainier than they?

So there it was: he was seventeen and Debbie was eighteen, and a fat chance there was of their getting married for ages and ages—if ever. Sometimes it made him feel so horribly depressed. He wondered whether she ever felt like that, too. And he had a nasty nagging feeling that perhaps she did not.

'Mr Layton tells me,' Ringer said, 'that they've got a lot of new routines. He says it's their best show ever.'

Angela gave another of those sniffs which Mark found so irritating. 'That wouldn't be saying a lot.'

Ringer let this remark pass. 'I wonder whether that young dark-haired girl is still with them. She seemed to be quite an up-and-coming star. You remember her, don't you, Mark?'

Again he answered offhandedly. 'Vaguely. She seemed a pretty good dancer, didn't she?'

'She's bound to be with them still,' Mrs Ringer said. 'She's Mr and Mrs Layton's daughter.'

'So she is,' Ringer said. 'I should have remembered.'

'Rather a pert type.' Mrs Ringer spoke disparagingly. She apparently had not been favourably impressed by the up-and-coming star. 'Very full of herself.'

'Well, if she's got talent—'

'You don't need much talent to shine in a lot like that,' Angela said. 'You just have to be the manager's daughter.'

'Oh,' Ringer said, 'I think there's more to it than that.'

What do they know about her? Mark thought. They're all talking about her and not one of them knows what she's really like. None of them knows her the way I do.

But he said nothing, and when the meal ended he went up to his study and sat down at the old worm-eaten desk where he worked on the correspondence course, but he was not working now; he was sitting there in the lamplight making doodles on a pad and thinking about Debbie.

There was some cheap faded paper on the walls of the room, but large areas of it were covered with photographs cut from newspapers and magazines. Some were pictures of his sporting heroes: Jack Hobbs, Walter Hammond, Harold Larwood, Dixie Dean, David Jack, Henry Cotton, Len Harvey, Kid Berg; Henry Segrave standing beside his record-breaking Sunbeam car on Southport Sands; Malcolm Campbell with his car on Pendine Sands; Lindbergh, Kingsford Smith, Amy Johnson...there were film stars too: Greta Garbo, Marlene Dietrich, Colleen Moore, Loretta Young...

But there was no place in this gallery for Deborah Layton. He had a photograph of her, but he would not have risked exhibiting it in that room; some other member of the family—his mother perhaps or Angela—might have walked in and recognized the subject. Then questions would have been asked and he would have had to lie; and nobody would have believed that he had no interest in a girl whose picture he displayed in his study. So it was better to let it remain hidden away and to see her here only with that inward eye which was for Wordsworth the bliss of solitude.

But very soon he would be seeing her again as she was in reality, a living, breathing, flesh-and-blood creature he could hold in his arms and love and love.

Oh, God: he thought. If only I could be with her always and for ever!

4 Storm in a Teacup

Mr Howard Layton arrived back in Heyworth from his publicity excursion to find himself face to face with a small crisis. When he came to think about it, it seemed to him that he spent much of his life these days facing crises of greater or lesser severity; the more severe usually being those of a financial nature. Cash flow, or rather the lack of it, was a recurring problem; in fact he never seemed to be free of it. Smaller audiences meant smaller income; yet expenses remained as high as ever; and if he tried to deal with the matter by increasing the price of the tickets there would be an inevitable decline in sales which might make the situation worse rather than better.

However, the crisis awaiting him on this occasion had nothing to do with money; it was of that awkward type which he generally categorised in his own mind as 'trouble in the company'. He sometimes thought it would have been easier to keep a party of children from bickering among themselves than a troupe of entertainers. Perhaps, being together so much of the time, they were bound to get on one another's nerves. And they could be so touchy; maybe it was the artistic temperament. If so he would have been glad to have a little less of it, because he was the one who always had to restore a semblance of harmony and keep the show from falling apart.

This time it was Dickie Wilson who was sulking in his room. He had locked the door and was refusing to come out. He was one of the younger members of the troupe, slim, elegant and quite good-looking. He did a song-and-dance act and anything else that was required of him. He confided in anyone who would listen to him that of course he was just filling in time with The Merrymakers until the right opening came along. Then he would be on his way up: the West End, films, you name it. Maybe he would try his luck in Hollywood when he had scraped together enough cash to make the journey. What did Fred Astaire have that Dickie Wilson hadn't got? In a way his ambitions were not much different from those of Debbie Layton.

The troupe was staying at The Anchor, which was a rather seedy temperance hotel and the cheapest accommodation available in Heyworth. In larger towns you could get digs with landladies who specialized in the theatrical trade, but in places like Heyworth and Braddlesham these useful creatures did not exist and you had to take whatever alternative there was.

The Anchor had been built in Victorian times and looked as though it still bore the original paint, which was a dirty brown in colour. There was a cobbled yard at the back where Layton parked the Morris, and when he walked into the hotel he was met by his wife, who was looking worried.

'Oh, Howard, I'm so glad you're back,' she said. 'There's been a bit of bother.'

'Bother! What sort of bother?'

'We'd better go in here,' Gloria said. She led the way into the lounge where Jackie Vernon and Maudie Maxted were installed at opposite ends of a long settee with their feet up, reading books. 'They can tell you. I didn't actually see it myself.'

'Didn't see what?'

'What happened.'

'Well, for God's sake, what did happen?'

39

Gloria looked at Jackie Vernon. 'You tell him. You saw it.'

Jackie closed the book but left a finger in it to keep the place. She was a rather languid young woman, tall, with black hair cut short like a man's and slicked back from her forehead. On stage she did male impersonations á la Vesta Tilley and also entertained at the piano.

Layton turned to her. 'Well?'

'There was a fight,' Jackie said.

'A fight? Who were fighting?'

'Dickie and Desmond.'

'Are you telling me they had a fight?' Layton could hardly believe it.

'Well, not exactly a fight. It didn't last all that long. Desmond punched Dickie in the eye. That's all.'

'What do you mean, that's all? It can't have been all. Where did this happen?'

'Right in here, darling. In front of our very eyes.' Miss Vernon spoke with a slight drawl which she had acquired with much practice. 'Quite shocking, it was.'

'But why did Desmond punch Dickie? There must have been something leading up to it.'

Maudie Maxted chipped in then. She

40

was a fluffy-haired blonde, pretty in a doll-like way, feather-brained but a competent dancer. She and Jackie always shared a room and possibly a bed too, though Layton never inquired into this; what they did in private was none of his business as long as it did not interfere with their work.

'It was the manager who started it,' Maudie said. She had a childish voice with a slight lisp. Layton saw that she was reading a novel by E.M Hull called *The Sheik,* but this was irrelevant.

'Mr Crane?'

Crane was the hotel manager, a weedy humourless man who sported a wig of such obvious falsity that Layton concluded it could hardly have been worn for cosmetic purposes and must have been used simply to keep the head warm. Crane's usual expression was one of deepest gloom, and whenever he appeared the temperature seemed to drop a degree or two.

'Yes, him,' Maudie said. 'Old laughing boy.'

Layton was rapidly losing patience. 'So will somebody please tell me how Mr Crane started a fight between Desmond and Dickie? Because I really would like to know.'

'He told Dickie it was against the rules to bring strong drink into the hotel.'

'Dickie did that?'

'Yes. He went out to get himself a drink somewhere and when he came back he had a bottle of whisky in his pocket. Crane happened to be in here when Dickie walked in, and of course he spotted it at once because the neck was showing. So he read the riot act.

' "Damn the rules," Dickie said, "and damn you, too, you miserable old bastard." Of course he'd had quite a few and didn't care what he said.'

'What did Crane do then?'

'He went quite red in the face, which made a change because as you know he usually looks like death warmed up. "You'd better mind your language, young man," he said. "And you'll please take that bottle out of this hotel." "Like hell I will," Dickie said; and he hauled it out of his pocket and clasped it to his chest as if it was a baby he was protecting.

'That was when Dorothy put her spoke in. She laid a hand on Dickie's arm and told him not to be a silly boy and cause trouble. "You know this is a temperance hotel," she said. "So why don't you do what Mr Crane says?" '

'She was here too?'

'Oh, yes. If she hadn't been I don't suppose things would have gone the way they did. You know how she always tries to keep the peace.'

Layton did. Dorothy was that kind of person. Desmond and Dorothy were a duo; in fact they were man and wife, Mr and Mrs Dring. They performed specialty dances, but they were a bit old for it now, though Dorothy still had a good figure and marvellous legs. They had been higher up the ladder, but now they were thankful to get any work, even with a troupe like The Merrymakers.

'Well,' Jackie said, taking up the story from Maudie, 'Dickie was in no mood to accept advice from her. He shook her hand off his arm and told her to mind her own business. "Why do you always have to shove your nose in where it's not wanted?" he said. "Go away, you interfering old cow".'

'Oh, dear!' Layton said. 'I don't like the sound of that.'

'Neither did she. She gasped a bit and drew away from him. And Desmond, who of course was there with her, his face went

43

all hard and he said: "You'll take that back and apologize." Dickie gave a sneer. "If you think I'm going to apologize to a couple of old has-beens like you two you've got another think coming." And that's when Desmond hit him.'

'In the eye?'

'Yes. It knocked him down. I'd guess he wasn't all that steady on his feet anyway, and it probably caught him off balance. He dropped the whisky bottle in falling, and Desmond picked it up, opened a window and threw it out into the yard, where it broke. Now Dickie's gone to his room and won't let anybody in, and he swears he's not going on stage tonight.'

'Oh, fine,' Layton said. 'That's just what we want. Where are Desmond and Dorothy?'

'In their room, I think. She went off in tears.'

'It was quite exciting for a while,' Maudie said. 'Just as well there weren't any other guests around at the time to see what went on.'

Layton thought it was lucky, too. But The Anchor was not the kind of hotel where guests hung around during the day if they had anything better to do.

'Well,' he said, with a sigh of resignation, 'I suppose I'd better go and see if I can sort things out.'

Dickie Wilson's room was on the first floor. Layton tapped lightly on the door with his knuckles and heard Dickie's voice.

'Go away.'

'It's me, Howard,' Layton said. He tried the door and found that it was indeed locked. 'Let me in, Dickie. I've got to have a talk with you.'

'I don't want to talk.'

'Now, don't be stupid. You know you can't stay in there for the rest of your life. We've got to work something out.'

There was no reply to this, but he heard the key turning in the lock, and then the door opened a little way and Dickie Wilson looked out at him. Layton could see that he had the makings of a black eye.

'I suppose you'd better come in then.'

Layton went in and Wilson closed the door. It was a dingy little room with the bare essentials of furniture and a wash-basin in one corner.

'I suppose you've heard what happened?'

'Yes.'

'I'm not going on, you know. Not tonight. Maybe never any more.'

'Now you're talking nonsense. Of course you're going on.'

'With an eye like this? I'll look a sight.'

'A bit of make-up and nobody will know.'

And maybe not care anyway, he thought. There was no theatre in Heyworth; they performed in the Oddfellows Hall, an old draughty building with accommodation for a couple of hundred or so people on hard chairs. It was a gloomy place in which to perform; enough to give you the willies; especially with perhaps only half the seats occupied. It was difficult to get a small audience going in a large hall; there was no cosiness about it. But it was the same everywhere; there was nothing like a full house to give you a feeling of confidence in yourself; it brought the best out of performers and audience alike to produce that magical accord between one side of the footlights and the other. It was all a double act when you really got down to it.

'I think you owe Dorothy an apology,' Layton said.

'It's Desmond who should apologize. He attacked me.'

'Only because you called his wife an interfering old cow.'

Wilson gave a sheepish grin. 'Did I say that?'

'So I've been told.'

'Well, it was none of her business.'

'Whether it was or whether it wasn't, you shouldn't have insulted her. She was only trying to help. Now you've hurt her feelings. Ladies of her age don't like to be reminded that they're not as young as they used to be.'

'Perhaps I did come it a bit strong,' Wilson admitted.

'So now you'll go and apologize, will you?'

'Only if Desmond apologizes to me.'

Layton gave a sigh of exasperation. It was like dealing with a set of kids. 'All right; I'll go and hear what he says.'

'Apologize to that worm!' Dring said. 'Never!'

Layton had found the Drings in their room. Dorothy had dried her eyes but she was not looking at all happy. Desmond had had time to cool down but he was still feeling resentful and unforgiving.

'Oh, come on,' Layton said. 'I'm sure he didn't really mean it. He'd been drinking, hadn't he?'

'*In vino veritas,*' Dring replied sententiously. 'That young man may find himself in real trouble if he goes on the way he's been doing.'

Layton thought there might be some truth in that. Dickie seemed to be getting a bit too fond of the bottle. And it wouldn't do; it just would not do.

'So what's it to be? Do we have mutual apologies and a show that goes on, or do we all stand on our dignity and have trouble all round?'

Dring glanced at his wife. 'What do you say?'

She said: 'I think you should do as Howard suggests. Dickie's not such a bad boy really. I'm sure he's sorry.'

Layton guessed that it was his hint regarding the show that had swayed her. She would not want to put the evening's performance in jeopardy. It was their living.

'Very well,' Dring said. 'I'll do it.'

So in the end it was a case of shaking hands and agreeing to forget the whole unfortunate incident. Layton thought of asking Wilson to go and apologize to Crane also but decided not to push him too far. Instead, he went to see the hotel manager himself and told him that Wilson was sorry for the way he had behaved and had promised it would not happen again.

Crane was huffy, but he had nothing to gain by making a fuss and it was not too difficult to persuade him to let the matter rest.

Debbie seemed to regard the incident as one huge joke. 'He was squiffy, of course. Anyone could see that.'

'So you were there too?' Layton said.

'Oh, yes. It was so funny. I had to laugh.'

'It wasn't really so very funny. It could have had unfortunate repercussions.'

She seemed unable to take the incident as seriously as he did. 'But it was all a lot of fuss about nothing. People are so silly. It was just a storm in a teacup.'

Layton supposed to her it was indeed no more than that. She was young; she never seemed to worry about anything. Perhaps it was as well; there would be plenty of time for worrying when she grew older.

And perhaps it was, as she had said, no more than a storm in a teacup. But there were too many of those storms for his liking. Maybe one day one of them would wreck the boat.

5 Marvellous Evening

Mark Ringer first saw Debbie Layton when he was fourteen years old and she was fifteen. It was when she was just starting to make an impression with the troupe. But at that time she made no impression whatever on him. Looking back, he failed to understand how he could have been so unaffected by her charms. A year later, when The Merrymakers again visited Braddlesham, he fell madly in love with her.

She seemed to have matured a lot in that year. He was sitting near the front, very close to the stage, and he could not take his eyes off her; he was fascinated by her every movement, every gesture, every turn of the head and flutter of the eyelids. He had imagined himself to be in love with girls before, but it had never been like this.

When the troupe moved on to Sawborough he cycled over there and saw the show again in the Jubilee Hall. He told no one

50

where he had been; he had no wish to be laughed at for falling in love with a dancer in a travelling company of entertainers. It was his secret, his alone.

He did not see her for another year. He thought about her every day at first, but as time passed she was less often in his mind and the mental image of her became blurred. Then it was autumn once more, and Howard Layton appeared in the village with his posters and complimentary tickets, and Mark waited with suppressed excitement for the moment when he would see her again. There was a trace of doubt mixed in with the joy of anticipation, a fear that one look at her might mean the end of it, that she would not be as he had remembered her, not the creature of his dreams but someone entirely different, a stranger for whom he had no feeling at all.

Perhaps it would be better that way; he would then be free of this enchantment, this dream of the unattainable; and his mind would be more at peace. But he knew that this was not what he wanted; he did not wish to be free from the witchery, the spell she had placed on him. He wanted it all to be just the same as before.

And it was the same. The moment she stepped on to the stage he knew it. Another year had matured her even more; at seventeen she was passing gracefully from adolescence into early womanhood. She had grown a little in height, but she was still not tall and probably never would be. She was slender and had beautiful legs, and everything about her delighted the youthful admirer, of whose existence she was as yet completely unaware.

He knew now without a doubt that he loved her, wanted her, longed for her. He wondered how he could get to speak to her, introduce himself to her. If this had been a London theatre and he had been a rich young man instead of an impecunious student he supposed he could have waited for her at the stage-door with a bouquet of flowers, and could have invited her to have supper with him in romantic and intimate surroundings. But this was just a scruffy village hall and there was no stage-door. And even if there had been he would not have dared to approach her; not here where he was so well-known and anyone might have seen him. It would have been all round the village in no time. What a subject for gossip! It made him feel hot under the collar just to think about it.

During the week that The Merrymakers stayed in the village he thought up a hundred schemes for speaking to the girl in secret and rejected them all as quite impractical. He had left Heyworth Grammar at the end of the summer term and was now working on the correspondence course; but he found it impossible to keep his mind on his studies while he knew that Debbie Layton was somewhere near. His imagination kept coming up with fantasies in which he and Debbie were lovers and he was rich and had taken her away from the stage because he wanted to have her all to himself. His favourite daydream had the two of them on a tropical island, uninhabited except for themselves. All they did was lie in the sun and swim in the lagoon and make love. It was paradise.

Unfortunately, it was only a paradise of the mind, and he had to come back to the reality that was this grubby little room with the flaking ceiling and the photographs pasted on the walls; had to come back to the knowledge that he had still not even spoken to the partner in his fantasy and that she knew nothing whatever of the passion for her that she had aroused in his heart.

When the company moved on to the next place on its itinerary, the small market town of Sawborough, he again rode over there on his bicycle and waited in the cold outside the Jubilee Hall until the members of the troupe left the building. The audience had already dispersed and he was rewarded for his vigil by a glimpse of Miss Layton under the light of a streetlamp. She had a beret on her head and her coat collar was turned up to her ears so that he could see only a portion of her face, a pale glimmer where the light caught it.

If she had been alone he might have summoned up the courage to accost her, but she was with some of the others of the party and it was out of the question. Someone must have said something funny, for he heard her give a little bubbling laugh which sounded full of the joy of life, and he felt a pang because he was excluded from that group of which she was a member. As far as they were concerned he was an outsider, and it pained him to realize it.

And then he suddenly decided that he just had to make a move, that he could not simply allow her to walk away out of sight. This was the closest she had ever been to him, and he had to keep her there if only for a few more moments.

'Excuse me,' he said.

They had almost gone past, scarcely noticing he was there; but now they halted and looked at him. There were four of them. One was the woman with the cropped hair who played the piano, and there was the one with the fuzzy blonde hair who did nothing in particular except join in the singing and dancing. There was also the young man who was such an agile dancer and did a bit of singing too. Mark recognized them all, though he did not remember their names. And of course there was Debbie.

'Yes?' the young man said, questioningly.

Mark was tongue-tied. He had made the initial approach, had stopped them dead in their tracks, and now he simply did not know what to say. He met Debbie's gaze for a moment, cool, perhaps faintly mocking. They were all watching him, waiting for him to say what he had to say; but it was of her that he was most acutely aware.

In desperation he said: 'You're Merry-makers, aren't you?'

The man said: 'The question is ambiguous. Do you mean merrymakers in general with a small m, or do you mean The Merrymakers, capital T, capital M?'

Mark felt foolish, and he did not care for the bantering way in which the man had spoken.

'I meant The Merrymakers, the concert party. You are, aren't you? In it, I mean.'

It was Debbie who replied. 'Yes, we are.'

They were the first words she had ever spoken to him. He felt sure they would be scorched on his mind for ever—in letters of gold.

'Well,' the man said, 'that's settled that. Was there anything else you wanted to say? Because if not, I think we'll be on our way. It's dashed chilly out here.' He gave a histrionic shiver as if to emphasize the point.

'I just wanted to say I think you're very good.' He was answering the man but his words were really addressed to one person only. He was looking at her when he spoke.

'A fan!' the man cried. 'A veritable fan,

by God! How awfully gratifying!' Still in that bantering style.

'So you saw the show?' Debbie said.

'Not here. I saw it at Braddlesham last week.'

'And you came all the way over here to tell us you like it?' She sounded amused.

'No, not exactly. I happened to be here and I saw the people leaving. So I waited.'

It seemed an unlikely story. If he had wanted to tell them how much he had enjoyed the show why had he not done so at the time, at Braddlesham? Why wait until he just happened to be passing the Jubilee Hall in Sawborough? But perhaps the unlikelihood of it would not occur to them. Perhaps they were not interested enough in him to give it a thought.

'It's a pity you weren't in the audience tonight,' Debbie said. 'You might have put a little life into them. They were all sitting on their hands.'

'I'm sorry to hear that.'

'What's your name?' she asked.

He told her, omitting the surname. 'It's Mark.'

'Come along,' the man said. 'We can't stand around here all night.'

He and the woman with the cropped hair and the blond one began to move away. The girl followed them, a little way behind. She had made only a few steps when she turned her head and said:

'Good-night, Mark.'

'Good-night, Debbie,' he said.

It seemed to startle her for a moment, that use of her name, though she must have guessed he would have seen it on the programmes. But then she gave a laugh and a little flutter of the hand and was hurrying to catch up with the others. They turned a corner and were out of sight.

He rode back to Braddlesham in a kind of daze. He could hardly believe that he had actually spoken to the girl, standing face to face with her and with no more than three or four feet of pavement separating them. And she had asked him his name and had said: 'Good-night, Mark.' And he had called her Debbie and she had laughed, as though it had pleased her, not minding at all.

How was that for a marvellous evening! An evening that in the end had passed all expectations. Now he was more in love with her than ever. And now she did not seem quite so far out of his reach.

The very fact that she had spoken to him brought her that much closer, that much more accessible. Hitherto she had been a kind of ethereal being, a creature far removed from the humdrum world in which he lived and moved; but now at a stroke all that was changed. She had, as it were, stepped across the barrier of the footlights and revealed herself as a normal flesh-and-blood person just as he was.

It began to rain when he was only half-way on the ride back to Braddlesham. By the time he reached home he was thoroughly drenched, but no amount of rain could dampen his spirits. It was late when he walked into the house and was greeted with a barrage of questions as to where he had been. His explanation that he had simply gone for a bike ride was received with incredulity.

'A bike ride! Until this hour!' his father said. 'Have you gone mad?'

Mark defended himself with energy. 'I have to take some exercise, don't I? I mean, after sitting at a desk all day I need it. For my health.'

'Well, I suppose that's true,' Ringer admitted with some reluctance. 'But don't you think this is overdoing it? Where did you go?'

'Oh, here and there.' He mentioned a number of villages. 'Matter of fact I lost my way in the dark. I didn't really mean to go so far.'

'We were worried about you,' Mrs Ringer said.

'I'm sorry. But there was no need. Really.'

Angela gave a smirk and said: 'I think he's been to see a girl.'

Mark turned on her sharply. 'You can think what you like.' She was closer to the truth than perhaps she had supposed. 'And it's none of your business what I do, so why don't you hold your tongue?'

'Oh, dear!' she said. 'Aren't we touchy!'

'Now you two,' Mrs Ringer scolded. 'Let's not have any of your bickering. And you, Mark, had better get those wet clothes off before you catch your death of cold.'

It was a good excuse for him to get out of the room where he had a feeling that Angela might have been ready to do some more probing. One thing was certain: he could not ride over to Sawborough again and wait for the people to come out of the Jubilee Hall. If he arrived home late a second time he would need a better explanation than that he had had lost his way again. He would have liked to have another glimpse of Debbie before The Merrymakers moved on from Sawborough and took themselves beyond his range, but he feared it would not be possible.

In fact a good nine months were to elapse before he saw her again, and then it was in a completely different place.

6   First Gift

Mr Ringer never had a real holiday; he could not trust anyone else to look after the business while he went away. So, apart from Sundays and Bank Holidays, he was hard at it all through the year. He was not, however, a selfish man, and he regularly sent his family away for a fortnight by the sea in August. He himself would join them for a short weekend in the middle of the their stay, travelling down on the Saturday evening and returning late on the Sunday, so that he was ready to open the shop on the Monday morning. It was not much of a break, but it made a change.

When Mark accompanied his mother and sister on their latest seaside holiday he had not seen Debbie Layton since that autumn evening in Sawborough outside the Jubilee Hall. Nor had he had any communication with her, though he had occasionally thought of writing to her; after all it was perfectly normal for stage performers to receive fan mail from complete strangers, and he could hardly be classed as a stranger now that he had spoken to her and told her his name.

But even if he had had the courage to write the letter he would not have known where to send it. The Merrymakers were forever on the move, never staying in one place for any length of time, and as far as he knew they had no permanent base to which he could have addressed the envelope; so in the end he abandoned the idea and resigned himself to the long wait until they next appeared in Braddlesham.

Yet now the image of the girl was more than ever in his mind. He dreamed of her by night and thought of her by day. He could not forget her, and indeed he had no wish to do so. He knew that older people, worldly-wise, might have shaken their heads if they had known about it; might have dismissed it as no more than a youthful infatuation which he would grow out of in time. But he knew better, knew that it was far more than that, was convinced of it. And still he told no one, keeping the secret strictly to himself.

They stayed at a third-rate private hotel known as Exley House, which could not even by the wildest exaggeration have been described as being a stone's throw from the beach. It was tucked away in a narrow side-street, some hundred yards or so behind the promenade and separated from it by a number of other buildings. It was indeed more of a boarding-house than a hotel, and the Ringers always used it because it was owned by a cousin of Mr Ringer's, a widow named Mrs Badger.

Mrs Badger was a large comfortable woman in her middle fifties; she had a lot of greying hair piled up on top of her head like a small beehive and she always wore black, as though in permanent mourning for her departed husband, whom she had in fact been thankful to be rid of, since in life he had been little better than a parasite, and a drunken one at that. She kept a framed photograph of the late Thomas

Badger in her bedroom, not so much, Mr Ringer maintained, in fond memory of the deceased but as an awful warning against being caught a second time.

As was usual at the height of the holiday season, Exley House had a full complement of guests and the Ringers were not favoured with the best of the rooms. The one allotted to Mark was on the second floor at the rear, and the window looked out on to an alleyway and the featureless wall of another building. He was not bothered by this uninspiring outlook, since he had expected nothing better. And indeed he anticipated no great enjoyment from this holiday, which was a kind of ritual that had to be gone through because it was expected of him. He had tentatively suggested that he might give it a miss this year and concentrate on his studies, but his father had refused to countenance any such break with tradition.

'Nonsense! You need a holiday like anyone else. All work and no play makes Jack a dull boy. Isn't that what they say?'

Mark was not interested in what they said, but he could see that he would not be allowed to drop out of the seaside holiday without a lot of argument, so he let it go.

'Besides,' Mr Ringer had said, 'your mother needs someone to carry the luggage and see to things on the journey. You're a young man now and it's your responsibility.'

So here he was, installed in a little back room in Exley House and already bored. He was on his own for a large part of the time; he had no desire for the company of his sister and his mother, and they amused themselves with activities that did not include him. Often in the morning they would play tennis on one of the public hard courts with hired rackets and balls, sometimes joining up for doubles with the Baileys, two sisters of about the same age as Angela who were staying with their parents at Exley House. Mark thought the Bailey family was a pain in the neck and did his best to avoid the girls, who often ogled him at meal-times and tried to waylay him in the corridors and strike up conversations.

'I believe Joan and Joy are sweet on you,' Angela told him. 'I can't imagine why.'

'Well, I'm not sweet on them,' Mark said. He regarded them as kids, far too young to interest him even if they had been much better-looking than they were.

'They're always talking about you. It's quite sickening really.'

His mother thought it would be nice if he made friends with the two Js, as he called them. 'They're such dear girls. I'm sure you'd like them if you got to know them better.'

'We'd have nothing to talk about. They haven't got the same interests as I have.'

'What interests do you have?' Angela asked.

Mark ignored the question. No discussion with Angela ever came to a satisfactory conclusion and he had learnt that it was best not to be drawn into an argument with her.

Mrs Ringer gave a sigh. 'Well, I suppose we can't make you do what you don't want to. It just seems such a pity, that's all.'

Mark failed to see why it was such a pity. It was not asking much to be left alone, was it? Why were people always so keen to get you to join in with whatever happened to please them?

It was on the third day that it happened. It was in the afternoon and he was strolling aimlessly along the promenade when he noticed someone sitting on one of the benches that were provided for anyone who felt like taking a rest. There was only one person sitting on this particular bench, and though she was not looking in his direction he sensed immediately that there was something oddly familiar about her, and it set his pulse racing. He was just a couple of paces away from her when she turned her head and he knew that his instinct had not misled him.

He came to a halt in front of her and she looked up at him with a slight frown. It was obvious that she did not recognize him and believed that she was about to be accosted by a stranger.

'Hello, Debbie,' he said.

She seemed startled. 'Who are you?' she asked. Very coldly; giving him no encouragement. She might have been saying: 'Go away and leave me alone.'

'Don't you remember me?' He was disappointed. She had been so much in his mind that he had almost come to believe that he must have been in hers, too. But of course it was not so. To her that one brief encounter would have meant nothing, an unimportant incident to be forgotten in a moment, lost amid all the other exciting business of living.

She shook her head. 'Should I? Have we met?' Still cool; still giving little encouragement.

'Last autumn. One evening outside the Jubilee Hall at Sawborough. After your show. You were there with three others from the company.'

'Oh,' she said; and he could tell that it had stirred her memory. 'Was that you?' Rather less cool now, perhaps.

'Yes.'

She took a closer look at him. 'You seem older.'

'I am older.' He was pleased that she had noticed the difference because he wanted to appear more mature, no longer a boy. And her words proved that she did remember him. 'Nine months older.'

'Yes,' she said, 'and so am I. We can't help it, can we?'

'I'm glad we can't.'

'Are you? You mean you want to grow old?'

'Not old; just older.'

'But it never stops, does it? Wouldn't it be nice if we could just say: 'Stop here. This is as far as I want to go'?

Though it would be difficult to decide exactly where to call a halt, wouldn't it?'

'I suppose it would.'

'Now,' she said, 'don't tell me your name. Let me see if I can remember.' Her forehead puckered slightly and her eyes were half-closed as she put her mind to the problem. He thought she too had matured in those months since he had last seen her. And of course he had never been as close to her as this in broad daylight; it was more revealing than the lighting in Braddlesham Clover Hall or the street-lamp outside the Jubilee Hall at Sawborough. But she had nothing to fear from the daylight; it revealed no previously hidden blemishes. In his eyes she was lovelier than ever. 'It wasn't Matthew, was it? No; I've got it now. Mark. Am I right?'

'Right,' he said.

She clapped her hands. 'Now wasn't that clever of me?'

'Yes, it was. I wouldn't have been at all surprised if you'd forgotten it altogether. I don't suppose it seemed at all important to you. That encounter, I mean.'

'Did it to you?'

'Oh, yes. I really had to screw up all my courage before I dared to speak to you.'

'To all of us, you mean?'

'No. The others were not important. It was you I wanted to speak to. It wasn't an accident, my being there just then. I'd biked over from Braddlesham on purpose and I'd been waiting for you to come out after the audience had all gone.'

'Really?' She seemed quite amazed by this revelation. But, he thought, not displeased. 'Really and truly?'

'Really and truly.'

'I think you'd better sit down,' she said; and she patted the seat beside her.

'You don't mind?'

'I've been bored,' she said. 'It'll make a change to talk to someone.'

Not to him in particular, he thought. Just someone. But perhaps not just anyone. There was a difference.

He sat down, not too close to her, leaving a gap between them. But not a large gap.

'What are you doing here?' she asked.

'I'm on holiday. With my mother and sister. We always come here in August.'

'Oh, I see.'

'Are you on holiday?'

'Not officially. We're in the show that's on at the Pier Pavilion.'

'You are? But I've seen the posters and there's no mention of The Merrymakers on them.'

'Of course not. We just make up the numbers. It's the sort of thing we do in the summer season. Then we go back to touring in the autumn.'

'So what did you mean by not being officially on holiday?'

'I meant that just at the moment I'm on the sick list, so I'm not working. That's why I spend my time here looking at the sea and counting the pebbles on the beach.'

He wondered whether she was kidding him. 'You don't look ill.'

'I'm not. I sprained my left ankle, and I haven't been able to go on stage since I did it.'

He glanced at her ankles. She was bare-legged and he could detect no difference between the left one and the right. There was no apparent swelling and she was not wearing a bandage of any kind.

'Is it still bad?'

'No, it isn't bad at all. I can walk quite well, but I've been ordered not to do any dancing for another couple of weeks just in case it goes again. Meanwhile, as you see, I'm a lady of leisure.'

He could hardly believe this was happening; that he was actually sitting beside her and talking to her. And the remarkable thing was that she appeared to be quite friendly now; there was no stand-offishness about her, and all the initial coolness had vanished. Indeed, it was almost as if they had known each other for years.

Then suddenly she said: 'Have you got any money?'

The questions took him by surprise; it was so unexpected. Surely she was not going to ask him for a loan. That would have been too disillusioning.

But he answered truthfully: 'A little.' His father had given him two pounds for pocket-money and he had some more that he had saved up. He had spent some of it, but not much. 'Why?'

'I thought you might like to buy me an ice-cream.'

'Oh,' he said, relieved. 'Why, yes, of course.'

She said she knew a café where they

served the most divine ices; and they went there and sat at a table eating these divine strawberry ices from long-stemmed silvery metal cups filmed with condensation on the outside.

'Aren't these just gorgeous?' she said.

'Yes, gorgeous.'

And you too, he thought, you too. And it was not a dream; it was real. And the reality took his breath away. How could he have come to be so lucky?

Later they strolled along to the Pleasure Beach and he took her on the Scenic Railway, which was a new experience for her. When they reached the top of the climb and the car went skimming down the other side she gave a scream and clutched at him. And then he put his arm round her and she let it remain there for the rest of the ride.

They stayed on for a second circuit, and he had never enjoyed the Scenic Railway half so much. It was a fine sunny day and the sea was calm, and from high up you could see for miles; you could see ships, apparently as motionless as rocks but with long banners of smoke coming from their funnels and masts sticking up like flagpoles. There were sails, too, and closer to the shore were pleasure-boats and a few strong swimmers who ventured out well beyond the shallows where the paddlers stayed.

After this they took a ride through the Tunnel of Fear, where skeletons suddenly appeared, rattling their bones and grinning at you, and in the darkness insubstantial things touched your face like invisible fingers.

Then it was the hoop-la stall, and he won a worthless trinket and gave it to Debbie. It was a mere nothing; yet it was his first gift to her and therefore significant in his eyes if not in hers.

Before they parted he tried to extract from her a promise that she would meet him again the next day; but she would not commit herself. The most she would say was that she might be on the bench at the same time, or she might not.

He had to be content with that. He was afraid she might already have tired of his company, and this was a depressing thought. He tried to banish it from his mind, but could not. He feared it was all over between them and that she would not be waiting for him the next day.

But in the event she was.

7 Sea Trip

It was a cooler day than the previous one, and when he approached the bench he saw that she was wearing a white polo-necked sweater. It was close-fitting and emphasized the shape of her small firm breasts.

'So you decided to come after all,' he said.

She gave a little shrug. 'I had nothing better to do.'

'How is your ankle?'

'It's all right.'

It certainly appeared to be. There was no sign of a limp as she walked beside him and he could only feel glad that it had not been decided that she was fit to go back to the dancing. Below them on the left was the beach with its scattering of deckchairs and wooden huts and square canvas tents in which the bathers left their clothes, and donkeys and here and there a boat drawn up on the sand. The North Sea looked less inviting this afternoon; it was grey and rather choppy and there were fewer swimmers venturing out into the deep water.

One of the touting photographers took a snapshot of them, and as they went past he thrust a card into Mark's hand. It bore the address of the shop where the photograph could be picked up. Mark put the card in his pocket and thought no more about it.

A little later it began to rain and they had to run to one of the glass-sided shelters.

'This would happen,' she said. 'Typical English summer weather. What do we do now?'

'I don't know.'

'Haven't you any suggestions?'

'I suppose we could go the pictures.'

She seemed a good deal less than enraptured with the idea, but she could think of nothing better and they went to a cinema called The Gem. The place was only about half-full and they found seats at the back, with empty spaces on each side of them. It was an old cinema and the auditorium was like a long narrow box with a gangway down the middle. They were sitting just below the window in the projector room, and the beam of light which carried the flickering images to the screen at the other end passed over their heads like a kind of intangible conveyor-belt. They had come in in the middle of a film and it was difficult to pick up the threads of the story. Mark was not trying very hard, because he was more interested in his companion than in any moving shadows on a silver screen.

After a while she leaned towards him and whispered: 'I don't think much of this, do you?'

'No,' he said. 'But at least it's dry in here.'

A little later he became aware that she was leaning towards him again. When he turned his head he discovered her face only a few inches from his. There was a kind of erotic influence about a cinema; it was not just what went 'on on the screen; it was in the atmosphere, the semi-darkness, the warmth, the very plush of the seats. He felt it then, and its effect was irresistible. He lowered his head and kissed the lips so invitingly close to his own.

It was not skilfully done; he was no expert in such matters and the kiss was a clumsy one. Even at the moment of contact he was appalled by his own temerity and half expected the girl to recoil from him. He was ready to apologize at once if she did so; though had she not herself invited the kiss? And in fact there was no need for any apology; for instead of drawing away from him she slipped an arm round his neck and held him there, her mouth pressed ardently to his and her lips opening like a sea-anemone.

He could feel the arm of the seat pressing into his side and a moment later she had taken hold of his left hand and guided it to her breast. He was not sure what she was wearing under the sweater, but it could not have been much and he could trace the rounded shape with his fingers and detect the small protuberance of the nipple at the centre. He was in a kind of intoxication of pleasure that was almost a delirium. But even while he was caught up in this enchantment he could not rid himself of an underlying sense of uneasiness. Because, although there were no seats behind them and no one in those adjacent on either side, even though the auditorium was plunged in that gloom which to newcomers entering from the daylight outside appeared to be almost complete darkness, and though presumably everyone would be looking towards the screen and not the back, nevertheless it was not a private place and he could not be certain that what he and Debbie were doing would go entirely unobserved. So even while he was absorbed in the sensual pleasure of this embrace he was at the same time wondering nervously whether he ought not to be making some move to extricate himself from it.

Yet he made no such move. He could hear the background music of the film and snatches of dialogue which failed to register on his mind except as a kind of gibberish without point or meaning, and still his lips remained pressed to Debbie's as though they had become glued there, and still the fingers of his left hand moved over the contours of that divine shape beneath the stretched fabric of the sweater.

In the end it was she who broke it up, just as it had been she who had initiated it. She took her arm from his neck, pushed him away from her and sat back in her seat, not even looking at him any longer. He had only the side view of her face and he could read no expression on it. She said nothing, and he wondered whether she was regretting her impulsiveness. He would have spoken to her but could think of nothing to say, and for the rest of the programme they sat almost in silence.

When they came out of the cinema it had stopped raining and the sun was shining.

'I'm hungry,' she said. 'Let's go somewhere and eat.'

So they went to a tea-shop and had a meal: buttered scones and cream-cakes and delicious macaroons. Neither of them mentioned what had happened in the cinema, though they talked freely of other things. But it was in his mind all the time, and maybe in hers also.

'What,' she asked, 'do you intend to do in life? You haven't got a job, I suppose?'

It was the first time she had shown any interest in that subject, and he wished he could have given a more promising report than that he was studying by correspondence for a Civil Service examination.

'Do you think you'll pass?'

'I really don't know. There's a lot of competition.'

'Are you brainy?'

'About average, I suppose.'

'It's not enough, is it? You need to be above average to get the plums.'

'That's true,' he admitted. And it depressed him.

'What does your father do?'

'He's a grocer.'

'You mean that shop in Braddlesham High Street? I've forgotten the name.'

'Ringer.'

'So you're Mark Ringer?'

'Yes.' It was odd that she had never asked him his surname and he had never thought to tell her. He had of course not been keen to tell her about the grocery, but it had been bound to come out in the end. He feared it was hardly likely to impress a girl like her. 'How about you? Have you got any plans for the future?'

'You bet your sweet life I have. I'm going to get on in the theatre. One day my name will be up in lights. I'll be a star.'

'I think you will,' he said. 'You've got what it takes.' And this also depressed him; because how could he hope to keep up with her? Even if he managed to get that Civil Service job he would still be in a different world from her. 'Yes, you're certain to get to the top.'

She looked pleased. Her eyes shone. 'Do

you really think so?'

'Of course. Anyone can see you've got talent. You're the star of that show you're in.'

'Yes, but it's not much of a show, is it?' She was frowning now, as though doubts had crept in. 'You have to be noticed by someone who matters. And people who matter in the theatre don't bother to look at tatty little companies like The Merrymakers. I have to go to London. Somehow I've got to get to London. It's the only way.'

'Well, I'm sure you'll make it,' he said. 'One way or another, you'll make it, Debbie.'

With a sudden impulsive gesture she reached across the table and put her hand on his. 'You're sweet, Mark. You know that? You really are sweet. I'm glad we met.'

He could have jumped up and danced for joy, but it might have attracted attention in that dinky little tea-shop with the bead curtains and the polished brass ornaments, so he restrained himself. But it was the nicest thing she had said to him and he had never been so happy.

They were together again the next day and it was becoming a habit. He was afraid they might encounter his mother and Angela, and he did not wish them to know about Debbie; but so far their paths had not crossed. And he had not seen the Js, either.

'Whatever do you do with yourself all day?' Mrs Ringer asked. 'We hardly see anything of you.'

'Oh, this and that. I manage to amuse myself.'

'Joan and Joy can't understand why you don't join us,' Angela said. 'They think it's funny.'

'Well, if it gives them a laugh, fine.'

'Not that kind of funny. Peculiar. You don't want people to think you're wonky in the head, do you?'

'I'm not wonky in the head,' Mark said, 'and I don't give a hoot what anybody thinks.'

But perhaps it was not so very far from the truth at that. Perhaps he was a trifle mad; for certainly he was madly in love. And that was a kind of insanity which could be both a delight and a heartache.

On that third day of their companionship they went down to the harbour and looked at the ships. In the season it would have been crammed with fishing-boats, but even at this time of the year there was plenty of activity. There were some vessels that had brought timber from the Baltic discharging their cargoes at the wharves on the other side of the river, and there were pleasure-steamers and a few sailing-craft and a clanking dredger and a Thames barge with a cargo of grain. Over everything there hung that curious tang which seemed to be made up from a mixture of tar and oil and fresh paint and mud and soot and fish and seaweed and a hundred other ingredients.

There was a paddle-steamer about to depart on a short trip round The Flinders, a sandbank some distance offshore, which was submerged at high tide and presented a hazard to shipping.

'Let's go,' Debbie said, 'I've never been on the sea.'

'You haven't?'

'No. Have you?'

'Oh, yes,' Mark said. He had in fact once been taken for a trip in this very ship, the *Eastern Queen,* but he did not tell her so. He tried to give the impression that he was quite an experienced sailor, which might raise his standing in her eyes. 'Often.' It was an exaggeration but an excusable one, he thought.

There was a wooden ticket-office on the quay. He bought tickets for the two of them and they went up the gang-plank and stepped down on to the scrubbed deck of the steamer. Quite a lot of people were already on board, some on a higher deck for which one had to pay extra. A little smoke was drifting from the funnel and they could feel the heat coming up through the open engine-room skylights.

Mark led the way to the stern where there was plenty of spare seating, and a few minutes later the order was given to cast off and the paddles began to turn. Slowly the steamer moved away from the quay and headed downriver.

He felt Debbie's hand on his arm. 'This is exciting, isn't it?'

'You think so?'

'Oh, yes. I'm so glad we came.'

The giant paddle-wheels were churning up the water as they revolved inside the paddle-boxes. One could see it running off the blades in foaming torrents.

'Suppose,' she said, 'the boat were to sink. What then?'

'It won't,' Mark said. 'Why should it?

The sea is calm and there aren't any rocks.'

'But just suppose it did. Can you swim?'

'Yes.'

'I can't.'

'You won't need to. Even if we did sink there are life-buoys and rafts.'

'Where are the rafts?'

'You're sitting on one. These seats are made to float and you can see the loops of rope to hang on to.'

'You know a lot about these things, don't you?'

'Well—' he said; not denying it.

'If I were a man,' she said, 'I think I'd like to be a sailor; to go round the world seeing all kinds of foreign countries. Wouldn't that be a grand life?'

'Yes, it would.'

'Haven't you ever thought of doing that?'

'Yes, I've thought about it. When I was younger I was set on going to sea.'

'But not now?'

'No, not now.'

'Why not?'

'Well, you'd want to be an officer, wouldn't you? Not just a seaman. And to qualify as a ship's officer you need to go to a nautical training college or something of that sort. And it costs a lot of money and—well, it just never worked out.'

'What a pity,' she said. 'You'd have looked nice in an officer's uniform. Peaked cap, gold braid and all that.'

He thought so too. It would have been something to impress her with. But it was never to be.

The steamer threshed its way downriver, past the wharves and transit sheds and the lifeboat house and the skeletal remains of an old ship rusting and rotting away on the mud. They came to the harbour mouth, with the jetty on one side where a row of patient anglers sat with their lines dangling in the water; and then they were in the gentle swell of the North Sea and the land was receding astern.

After a while the steamer turned to port and headed northward, and from the deck the beach was visible, with tiny figures moving about on it; and later still they turned to starboard and came round to the eastern side of The Flinders which now formed a long low bank between the ship and the shore. It was almost low tide and the sands were well out of the water; they could see the bell-buoy and a lot of seals basking in the sun, which Debbie was thrilled to observe. Soon after that they were heading back towards the harbour mouth and the sea trip was nearly over.

When the paddle-boat had returned to its berth and the passengers were making their way ashore Mark suddenly spotted the Baileys, Mr and Mrs and the two girls, Joan and Joy. They were coming down the steps from the upper deck where they had been hidden from his view. He turned away pretty smartly, wondering whether they had seen him, and he gripped Debbie's arm to hold her back from the gang-plank.

'Wait her a minute. There are some people I know just going ashore. I'd rather they didn't see us.'

'What people?'

'They're staying at the hotel. I can't stand them. Man and wife and two girls.'

She was looking curiously at the departing passengers. 'Oh, I think I see them. They've just reached the quay.'

'Are they looking this way?' he asked, keeping his back turned in that direction.

'No. They're walking away now.'

He risked a glance and caught sight of the backs of the departing Bailey family and breathed a sigh of relief. He felt sure they had not seen him; if they had they would almost certainly have come over and spoken to him. And of course they would have told his mother that they had seen him with a young lady; they would never have been able to keep such a titbit to themselves. And then he would have had to do some explaining, which he did not wish to do.

It had been a close shave.

He spent the whole of the evening with Debbie and it was late when they parted. He kissed her and she clung to him for a while as if reluctant to let him go. It was quite a passionate embrace and it set his pulse racing again.

That night his dreams were full of her.

8 Nothing Foolish

He decided to get the snapshot from the photographer's shop and he bought a print for Debbie as well. She accepted it with no particular show of pleasure..

'We look like a pair of idiots,' she said.

Mark did not agree, and he doubted whether she really thought so, either. In his opinion it was a pretty good photograph. It had frozen her just as she was turning her head to speak to him, and it had caught the way she moved, the way she looked, the sheen of her hair, the very essence of her. This was the Debbie he knew, the Debbie he loved; and the fact was that he did not seem so out of place beside her, either. They looked as though they belonged together, an attractive young couple; there could be no doubt about it.

He wondered whether it might not be a good idea after all to introduce her to his mother. That was supposing she wished to be introduced. He suggested it to her, tentatively, and she turned it down flat.

'No.'

'Why not?'

'Because it would only spoil things.'

'In what way?'

'Oh, all sorts of ways. It's better as it is. Just you and me. No one else.'

Perhaps she was right at that, he thought. His mother would want to know all about her and might not be impressed to discover that she was one of The Merrymakers, a girl she had seen on the stage at the Clover Hall. And there would be Angela making sarcastic remarks which would infuriate him. Better to leave things as they were. The secrecy made it more romantic. Like Romeo and Juliet.

For her part Debbie had never suggested presenting him to her father and mother and the other members of the troupe. He was not sure whether this was because she was ashamed of him or whether she simply could not be bothered. He was rather glad; he felt that he would have been somewhat intimidated by Mr Howard Layton.

So they agreed to leave matters as they were. But oddly enough that afternoon she said she would like to see the hotel where he was staying.

'It is a hotel, isn't it?'

'Of a sort. It's owned by an aunt of mine. Mrs Badger.'

'Badger!' She gave a laugh. 'Don't tell me it's a hole in the ground.'

'It's a hole all right, but not in the ground. It's not worth seeing.'

However, she was not to be put off; she was strangely insistent that he should take her to see it. After some consideration, therefore, he decided that it would be all right to take her there. At that time of day there was unlikely to be anyone around to see them; the guests would all be out and Aunt Alice would be taking her usual afternoon nap. They could just go along, snatch a quick look at the outside of Exley House and come away again. No harm was likely to result from the visit.

'All right,' he said. 'If that's what you want let's go.'

He could tell that she was not very impressed with it when they got there, but he had not been expecting anything else. It was not the kind of place to impress anyone; not favourably anyway. The frontage was of plain brick and the window-frames were painted a sombre brown. There were three stone steps leading up to the entrance, with some rusty iron railings on each side. The door, which was standing open, was painted the same gloomy colour as the windows, and above it in bilious yellow lettering was the title of the establishment: EXLEY HOUSE.

'Well,' he said, 'that's it. I hope you're satisfied. Shall we go now?'

He was impatient to be gone from there, but she seemed to be in no hurry. She was gazing up at the higher windows.

'Which is yours?'

'Which is my what?'

'Your window.'

'None of those. My room is at the back.'

'Show me.'

He stared at her. 'You mean you want to see my room?'

'Of course.'

'But that's impossible. I mean—'

'Nonsense. What's so impossible about it? All you have to do is lead the way.'

'But there's nothing to see. It's just a room.'

She looked at him. 'Please, Mark.'

He saw that this was something else she had set her mind on; perhaps it had been her intention from the start. And again he gave in to her insistence.

'Very well.'

He went in front of her up the steps and into the hotel. There was a small entrance hall or lobby and a reception desk on the left, with a bell. Nobody was at the desk and there was no one in the cubby-hole of an office behind it. The staircase was straight ahead.

'Come on,' he said, keeping his voice low.

They went up two flights, meeting no one. He walked along a short passageway with the girl following and came to the door of his room. He opened it and they went inside and he closed the door behind them.

'So this is it?'

'This is it.'

Her glance travelled round the room, and it did not take long on the journey. Then she moved to the window and peered out.

'Lovely view!'

'It's the best I can offer you.'

She gave a laugh and drew the curtains, shutting out the daylight and leaving the room in shadow.

'Why did you do that?' he asked.

For answer she came to him, put her arms round his neck and kissed him. His response was immediate and for a while they clung to each other. Then she pushed him away.

'Lock the door.'

He hesitated uncertainly and she repeated the command with increased urgency.

'Go on. Lock it.'

He gave a shrug, walked to the door and turned the key in the lock. When he looked at her again he saw that she had kicked off her shoes and was stepping out of her skirt. He stared at her.

'What are you doing?'

'Undressing, of course.'

'But—'

'Look,' she said, 'you want to make love with me, don't you?'

'Of course I do, but—'

'So take your clothes off. Don't be stupid, Mark. We can't do it properly with our clothes on.'

He had never expected things to go as far as this. Even when she had asked to see his room it had not occurred to him that this was what she had in mind. But now that it had come to the point he was delighted. For of course she was right; it was what he wanted; what he wanted above all else.

That this was happening in Exley House of all places, that drab depressing pile of bricks and mortar, was scarcely believable. He had a vision of Aunt Alice Badger sternly disapproving, but he dismissed it, cast it from him with disdain. He did not care what she might have thought; he cared for nothing but the delirium of the moment.

When the girl was standing there naked he caught his breath. Even in the dimness of that darkened room he could see the charming contours of her youthful body: the rounded breasts, the perfectly proportioned arms and legs, the slender waist, the secret triangle below...

'You're beautiful,' he whispered. 'You're the most beautiful thing in the world.'

She laughed and struck a pose, one hand partly covering her breasts, the other shielding that secret part of her, as in a painting of Venus by an old master. It was done with a kind of self-mockery, a pretence of modesty; but she was smiling at him all the while, invitingly, bewitchingly.

'Beautiful! So beautiful!'

She laughed again and moved towards the bed.

There was no sound in the place when they left the room and went down the stairs. There was a characteristic odour about that house. All old houses had their own peculiar smells, but he felt sure he would remember this one always because it would be forever linked in his mind with the unforgettably rapturous hour he had spent with Debbie in his room.

They would have made it longer, stretching out this dream of delight to immeasurable lengths. But he knew that soon people would be returning. Aunt Alice would awake from her sleep and Exley House would come to life. He wanted to be gone before that happened; he did not wish to be seen with Debbie creeping down the stairs like two guilty intruders.

They met no one on the stairs, but just as they were leaving the lobby he thought he heard a sound behind him; it might have been a door closing. He glanced back but could see no one, and he concluded that he had imagined it. A moment later they were out of the building and walking briskly away.

When he returned to the hotel that evening he was intercepted by his mother as he was about to climb the stairs.

'I want a word with you,' she said.

He thought this sounded ominous, but he tried to appear unconcerned. 'A talk with me! About what?'

'I think,' she said, 'we had better go to your room. It will be more private.'

'All right.'

As they went up the stairs to the second

floor neither of them spoke a word. Mark had a pretty shrewd idea of what the subject of the talk would be, and he was apprehensive. He had never enjoyed having arguments with his mother; she always seemed to have the best of them. It was easier to deal with his father than with her; Alfred Ringer was far more easy-going than his wife.

When they walked into the room Mark saw her glance at the bed, and there was a certain tightening of the mouth, although she made no remark. He had straightened the quilt before leaving, but he was uneasily aware that it did not have quite the tidy appearance it had had after the chambermaid had operated on it in the morning.

There was only one chair and he offered it to his mother, but she declined it.

'I prefer to stand.'

He remained standing also; uncomfortable, ill-at-ease.

'Aunt Alice tells me,' Mrs Ringer said, 'that you brought a girl to this room this afternoon.'

'Aunt Alice! But—'

'Oh, she didn't see you herself. One of the maids caught sight of you leaving with this young person and reported it to your aunt.'

So he had been right in thinking he heard a noise; it had not been imagined. There had been someone watching him and Debbie as they left the hotel.

'You are not going to deny it, I suppose?'

It would have been pointless to do so; he would not have been believed.

'No,' he said.

'I suppose it was the same girl you were with on the paddle-boat yesterday?'

He was startled and he showed it. He wondered how she knew about that. And then he guessed the answer.

'So the Baileys did see me?'

'Yes.'

'And had to tell you, of course.'

'Mrs Bailey did. She wondered if I knew.'

'Nosey old thing.'

'Now, Mark! I won't have you saying things like that.'

'Well, it was none of her business.'

'She just thought I ought to know how you were spending your time.'

'You didn't say anything to me.'

'I was waiting for you to volunteer the

information yourself.' Mrs Ringer wore a pained expression like someone who felt she had been badly treated. 'I thought you might introduce the young person to me. After all, I am your mother. Surely it wouldn't have been too much to expect. Why didn't you?'

'Oh, I don't know. We just thought it didn't seem necessary.'

'You wouldn't be ashamed to let me see her, would you?'

'Of course not. What makes you say that?'

'It's just that Mrs Bailey wasn't very favourably impressed by the look of her.'

'She said that?'

'More or less. I forget the exact words.'

In fact Mrs Ringer had not forgotten them; they remained quite clearly in her memory. What Mrs Bailey had said was that the young lady looked like somebody who was no better than she ought to be. And Mrs Ringer knew very well what that meant.

'So Mrs Bailey wasn't very favourably impressed, was she?' Mark said. 'Well, I can tell you that the girl I was with looks a whole lot better than the two objects she has for daughters. Though of course that doesn't take much doing.'

'Really, Mark! That's not at all a polite thing to say. Joan and Joy may be a trifle plain, but they're very nice girls. A pretty face isn't everything, you know.'

And oh, how true that was, he thought. But he said nothing.

'So who is she?' Mrs Ringer asked.

'Just a girl I met. She's here with her parents.'

'And you've met them?'

'No.'

'I suppose that didn't seem necessary either?' Mrs Ringer was being mildly sarcastic. 'And what is her name?'

He had been expecting this question and he had a name ready on his tongue.'

'Louise.'

'Louise who?'

'Johnson.'

'Well,' Mrs Ringer said, 'I think you should bring this Louise Johnson along and introduce her to me. I should very much like to meet her.'

'I'm afraid that won't be possible.'

'Why not?'

'The Johnsons are leaving tomorrow morning.'

Mrs Ringer looked faintly suspicious.

'You're quite sure of that?'

'Of course I'm sure. We've already said goodbye.'

'In that case I suppose there's nothing to be done about it. A pity. I should have liked to see her. You know, of course, that you ought not to have brought her to your room. Your Aunt Alice is very strict about that sort of thing.' She glanced again at the bed. 'I hope you didn't—' She hesitated and her face reddened, as though she had been embarrassed by the thought that had come into her mind. Then she said with a rush, like someone taking a run at an obstacle: 'I hope you didn't do anything foolish.'

'No,' Mark said. 'Nothing foolish.'

9 Bonus

'We were seen,' Mark said.

'Were we?' Debbie said. 'On the boat or at the hotel?'

'Both.'

It was Saturday; the day when the fictitious Johnsons were supposed to be departing after their seaside holiday. But the genuine Miss Layton was still very much in evidence.

'So I suppose your mother knows all about us now?'

'Not all. There are some things it's better she doesn't know.'

Debbie gave a conspiratorial kind of smile. 'I can imagine.' She did not seem to be at all bothered by his revelation.

'She may have suspicions, of course. She kept glancing at the bed when she was talking to me about what she had been told. But she can't be sure.'

'Did she ask you who I was?'

'Naturally.'

'And you told her?'

'I told her your name was Louise Johnson and you were here with your parents. She said she'd like to meet you.'

'What did you say to that?'

'That it was impossible because the Johnson family were leaving this morning.'

She looked at him admiringly. 'What a wonderful liar you are, Mark darling.'

'I don't enjoy telling lies,' he said. 'I did it for you.'

'So I'm to blame?'

'All along the line. For everything. And I love you for it.'

'You're an idiot, Mark.'

'Yes,' he said, 'I know. But I don't mind if you don't. I'd rather be an idiot and loved by you than a genius and not.'

'There you go again. And suppose we're seen together another time? Your mother will know you've been lying.'

'I shall just have to tell her it's a different girl. She won't know; she never saw Miss Johnson.'

'But if it's those Baileys who see us, they'll know.'

'We shall just have to be careful then.'

She squeezed his arm. 'It's fun, isn't it?'

He guessed that she enjoyed the element of intrigue which lent an added piquancy to the affair. It was a game to her; and perhaps that was all it was. But to him it was no game; he was too deeply in love with her not to take it seriously. He wondered whether she really loved him; she had never told him she did, but perhaps she did not consider it necessary to put into words what her actions so fully demonstrated.

'Do you know what starts on Monday?' she asked.

'No. Anything special?'

'It is a bit special. It's Race Week.'

'Oh, is it?' He was not much interested.

'Why don't we go one day?'

The suggestion startled him slightly. He had never set foot on a racecourse. In his family people who went to the races and bet on horses were looked at rather askance. If they were not regarded quite as criminals they were certainly thought of as a bit fast and even somewhat immoral.

'I didn't know you were a racegoer.'

'I'm not,' she said. 'I've never been to a race-meeting in my life. I just thought it would be something different and exciting to do. A new experience. But of course if you don't want to—'

'Oh, it's not that.' He was prepared to do anything she wanted, even if it meant going to the races; but there was a snag: he had scarcely any money left. He had been paying for everything and she had been perfectly willing to let him do so. He was not sure whether or not she had any money of her own, and he would not have dreamed of asking; but his own little stock had gradually dwindled away until he was now down to the last shilling or two. And you needed money if you went to the races, didn't you? He was not sure whether you had to pay to go in, but he was sure Debbie would not be content just to watch the horses running. She would want to do some betting; that was the real excitement.

'So what is it?' she asked.

'I'm practically broke.'

'Oh!' she said; and he could tell that this was something that had simply not occurred to her. She was pouting slightly, like a child denied some treat. It was an engaging little pout but it was evidence of her displeasure and he regretted that he should have been the cause. If only he had been rich!

But then she smiled. 'Well, that's all right. You can get some from your mother, can't you?'

Mark thought that was doubtful. His mother was not particularly open-handed at the best of times, and he was afraid that at the moment he was not in her good books. If he asked her for money she would want to know precisely what he wanted it for, and he could hardly tell her it was to take Debbie to the races and maybe back a horse or two.

But then he had a better idea.

106

'I won't need to try. My father will be here this evening and I'll ask him. I'm sure he'll let me have some of the old spondulicks.'

She clapped her hands. 'Good-o!'

'There's one thing, though. I'm afraid I shan't be able to meet you tomorrow. While my father is here I'll be expected to be with the family. Sorry.'

'Oh, that's all right,' Debbie said. 'I couldn't have met you anyway. As it's a Sunday I'll have to be with my lot. It'll be horribly dull, but that's how it is.'

He was pleased to hear her say how dull it would be. There was an implication that life in his company was not dull. For him, of course, being with her was a delight all the way; it was all he asked for. He hated to think of the end of the holiday, just one week hence. After that there would be an emptiness in life, all zest gone.

How could he live without her?

It was not until the next day that he was able to speak to his father in private. Then he came to the point straightaway, because there was no sense in beating about the bush.

'I wonder if you could let me have a bit more money, Dad?'

Mr Ringer gave a little smile. They were in Mark's room, into which he had managed to entice his father.

'So you've emptied your purse in one week, have you?'

'Afraid so.'

'These young ladies can be expensive items, can't they?' Ringer said, with a twinkle in his eye.

'So you've heard about that?'

'My dear boy, you didn't imagine I wouldn't hear about it did you? It was dinned into my ears as soon as I got here. No other subject seemed to be of any importance.'

It was only to be expected, Mark thought. His father had to be told about his conduct—or misconduct, as some people would have called it.

'Your mother and your aunt really seem to have been quite upset about it.'

'I don't see why.'

'No? Different viewpoint, you see. That's what it is. Different viewpoint.'

'Has it upset you?' Mark asked.

'Now, now! I don't think that's a question you ought to ask your father.'

Which meant that it had not. Mark felt a sudden rush of affection for this undistinguished little man and would have hugged him if he had not known how embarrassing such a display of emotion would have been for both of them.

'What kind of girl was she?' Mr Ringer asked. 'Pretty?'

'Yes.'

'Think I'd have liked her?'

'I'm sure of it.'

'But I understand she's left.'

'Yes.'

'Expecting to see her again?'

'I don't know. I think it's unlikely.'

'Where do the Johnsons live?'

'Oh, miles away. Up north. Manchester.'

He was lying again, and he was enjoying it even less this time because he knew that his father would never doubt his word. Debbie had admired him for his lying, but there was really nothing admirable about it. It was despicable and he hated having to do it, but he could see no other way now.

'So,' Mr Ringer said, 'you won't be able to ride over on your bike.'

'Hardly.'

'Never mind. Maybe the Johnsons will

be here again next year and you'll see her then.'

'Yes, maybe.'

But who knew what might happen in a year's time? At his age a year was like an eternity. Though of course he would not have to wait as long as that to see the girl again, because she was not in Manchester but here, and her name was not Louise Johnson but Deborah Layton.

'So you need some more spending money,' Mr Ringer said.

'I don't like asking, but if you could just—'

'Yes, I know. It's like holding out the begging bowl, isn't it? Though I don't think the beggars are ever at all reluctant to do it. I reckon it's something you get used to.'

He was feeling in his breast pocket, and he pulled out a wallet and took two pound notes from it. These he handed to Mark, and then, as if by way of an afterthought, he added the bonus of a ten-shilling note.

'Thanks, Dad,' Mark said. 'This is very generous.'

'I know it is; and I don't suppose

you deserve it. Just don't throw it all away on fast women and slow gee-gees, that's all.'

He gave a laugh to show that this was meant as a joke. Mark laughed too, though his laugh was a bit forced. Unwittingly, Mr Ringer had got rather too close to the truth for comfort.

'No need to mention this to your mother,' he said. He laid a finger on the side of his nose and winked. 'Just between you and me, eh?'

He left late in the afternoon on his way back to Braddlesham and the treadmill of the grocery shop. In a way Mark was sorry to see him go, but it was better that way; if he had stayed on he would have expected to have his son's company for much of the time, and that would have made things difficult.

Mark, with two pound notes and a ten-bobber in his pocket, felt rich. Now he would be able to take Debbie to the races and there would be enough money to make a few modest bets. Nothing extravagant, of course, but enough to make her happy. And who knew? They might even strike a winning streak and come back loaded.

10 Day at the Races

They went to the races on the Tuesday. It was not one of the famous racecourses like Newmarket or Goodwood or Ascot, but there were all the things that Mark had always associated in his mind with such venues for the sport of kings. There were bookies and tick-tack men and white railings and quite an imposing grandstand; and there was a certain atmosphere, difficult to describe. Football grounds had their distinctive atmosphere too, but this was quite different; he felt it immediately and it excited him even before he had seen a horse or a jockey.

He was sure that Debbie felt it too. She squeezed his arm and said: 'Isn't it wonderful, Mark? Aren't you glad we came?'

He was. Only the faintest twinge of conscience reminded him that this was what he had always been led to believe was a scene of wickedness, of decadence and vice. Somehow it did not seem like that; it seemed like a lot of happy people having a day of harmless enjoyment in the summer sunshine.

It really was a delightful day; hot enough but not too hot, and hardly a cloud in the sky. Not all was innocence and light, of course. For a start there were the tipsters; seedy-looking men who offered to mark your card or give you a horse—at a price. The horse was apparently stowed away in a sealed envelope which was thrust at you with a knowing wink and a nod. Mark, new to all this, might have been persuaded to buy one of these remarkably thin horses, but Debbie was having none of it.

'Buzz off!' she said. 'Buzz off, you parasites!'

Amazingly, they did buzz off. Perhaps they recognized a young lady who was more than a match for them when they saw one.

'What do they take us for?' Debbie said. 'A pair of boobies? If they really knew which horses were going to win they'd get rich by backing them for themselves. They're just a set of confidence tricksters.'

'Well, you certainly knew how to deal with them,' Mark said admiringly. 'Are

113

you sure you haven't been to a race-meeting before?'

'Quite sure. But I know when I'm being conned. I wasn't born yesterday.'

He wondered whether she was really as worldly-wise as she would have had him believe. He hoped not. He would not have wanted her to be too sophisticated. But he supposed that in moving around with a troupe of professional entertainers you were bound to learn a thing or two about life.

When he had bought a race-card they started picking horses to back. Neither of them knew a thing about form, and the horses were just names to them. Very peculiar at that, some of them.

'I wonder how they think them up,' Mark said. 'Do they have any special meaning, do you think?'

'Possibly. But what's it matter? They're just names anyway.'

Nevertheless, it was on these that she chose which horses to back; if she liked a name it would make no difference to her what the odds were against that particular horse. Mark had a different system; he avoided the favourite because you could win little on them and he ruled out the rank outsiders because they obviously stood a very poor chance of being among the leaders. Instead he would pick a horse nearer the middle of the list, something at about five or six to one.

In the event neither system seemed to pay. Mark placed the bets with a bookmaker calling himself Honest John; two shillings for his own choice and the same for Debbie's. After three races had been run he found himself twelve shillings out of pocket. Debbie had lost nothing because he had been putting up her stake as well as his own. Not that she appeared to be any the less disappointed for that.

'What rotten luck,' she complained after the third race. 'If Happy Harry had won I'd have pulled in five pounds. It was fifty to one.'

'It was fifty to one because it didn't stand a chance,' Mark said. 'That's the way things work.'

'So you know all about it?'

'No, I don't know all about it. But it stands to reason that the poorer a horse is the longer the odds are against it. It's plain logic.'

'Well,' she said, 'your horse didn't win either, so you can't brag.'

115

'I'm not bragging. I always did think betting on horses was a mug's game. Now I'm sure of it.'

It was not really much of a spectacle either in his opinion. There were so few races and they were finished so quickly. There was a flurry of hoofs; you caught a glimpse of brightly coloured shirts and flaring nostrils, the jockeys standing up in the stirrups and urging their horses on to greater effort; and then they were gone. It was impossible even to tell which horses had won until the numbers went up in the frame. He would rather have watched a cricket match any day.

They were strolling about after the third race when someone said: 'Well, if it isn't Miss Layton!'

An elegantly dressed man had come to a halt in front of them and raised his hat. He was accompanied by an attractive young woman wearing a wide-brimmed hat and a flowered dress. She was carrying a parasol.

Debbie seemed startled at hearing herself addressed by name. She looked at the man for a moment, as though not recognizing him; but then she smiled.

'Why, it's Mr Crowther.'

'None other. This is an unexpected pleasure. Are you, as they say, resting?'

Debbie smiled. 'In a way. I'm recovering from a sprained ankle. The others are appearing at the Pier Pavilion. I'll probably join them against next week.'

'Ah!' Crowther said. 'That explains it all.'

He appeared to be about thirty; black-haired, with a narrow face, a rather prominent nose, thin lips and slightly hooded eyes that gave him a sleepy look. He was somewhat above average height and there was an air of languor about him which might have been more assumed than natural.

He turned to his companion. 'Lavinia, my dear, allow me to introduce you to Miss Deborah Layton, who by a remarkable coincidence happens to be in the same profession as yourself.'

'Really?' The woman with the parasol treated Debbie to a cool and rather disdainful glance.

'Yes, really. She's with a company called The Merrymakers.' Crowther looked at Debbie for confirmation. 'I have got it right, haven't I?'

'Yes, quite right.'

117

'Miss Montague,' Crowther said, indicating his female companion, 'is on the London stage. That is to say she is when she's working. At the moment Mr Cochran doesn't appear to require her services, which leaves her free to come to the races.'

Mark gathered from this that Lavinia Montague was a chorus girl. He would have made a guess that the name was strictly professional and that her real name was somewhat more plebeian. She appeared not to be at all pleased by the rather chaffing way in which Crowther had introduced her, and she showed her displeasure by a slight frown and a tightening of the lips. She had a small pouting mouth outlined with bright red lipstick.

Crowther now turned his attention to Mark, who had been left out of the initial introduction. 'And are you also a member of The Merrymakers?'

Before Mark could answer Debbie said quickly: 'Oh, no; he's just a friend. His name's Mark Ringer.'

Crowther gave Mark a keener look. 'Haven't I met you somewhere?'

'Yes,' Mark said. 'On the cricket field.'

He had recognized Hugh Crowther at

once as the owner of Longmere Hall, a country house less than a mile from the village of Braddlesham. There was a cricket ground on the estate and the Braddlesham club was allowed to use it when it was not required by the owner. There was a regular fixture when the village team played Mr Crowther's eleven, a side gathered by him from amongst his friends and acquaintances. It was earlier in the summer when Mark had played for Braddlesham in the annual match and had in fact knocked up a half-century.

'Why, of course,' Crowther said. 'I remember now. Quite a batsman, aren't you?'

Crowther was a pretty mediocre player himself, but he liked to get into his white flannels and cricket boots now and then. The cricket ground had not been laid out by him; it had been there for many years before he bought the estate, and he was not as highly respected in the neighbourhood as the previous owner had been. The fact was that he was not considered a proper gentleman; not like his immediate predecessor, who had always been referred to as the Squire. But Squire Langford had died, leaving the estate in a financial mess, and it had been acquired by Hugh Crowther.

The basic facts about Crowther were fairly well known. He was the son of a north country mill-owner who had made a fortune from nothing and had been able to send his only child to a public school. But Hugh had proved something of a disappointment, preferring the life of a wealthy playboy to that of a hard-working industrialist. When his father died he was still in his early twenties and quite incapable of taking control of a factory employing some five hundred workers. However, a satisfactory arrangement was devised whereby the company was run by a hard-headed Yorkshireman and Hugh became in effect little more than a sleeping-partner. In return for an undertaking not to interfere with the day-to-day running of the business he was given a generous capital sum and a yearly allowance which was sufficient to keep him in the style of life which most appealed to him.

In addition to Longmere Hall he owned a house in London, and he flitted back and forth between these two as the spirit moved him. He was not married and it was said that he entertained lavishly at the hall, where his guests were likely to include numbers of attractive young women brought down from London.

Mark was not sure how accurate these stories were, but he had the evidence of Miss Lavinia Montague in person, and she seemed to confirm the truth of what he had heard.

'I have a suggestion,' Crowther said. 'Why don't you two young people join my party, eh?' The invitation was made to include both of them, but it was at Debbie that he was looking as he spoke. 'Wouldn't that be a splendid idea?'

Mark glanced at Miss Montague and it was evident that she for one did not think it was at all a splendid idea. He was inclined to agree with her; he had no desire to join forces with Hugh Crowther or anyone else; he preferred to have Debbie to himself.

'Oh,' he said, 'I don't really think—'

But Debbie stopped him before he could finish. 'Why,' she said, 'that would be lovely, wouldn't it, Mark?'

'Well, I don't know.'

'Of course you do. Thank you, Mr Crowther. We'd love to join you.'

'Call me Hugh,' Crowther said. 'No

formality between friends. Come along then.'

The other members of the party turned out to be just two people, a man and another young woman. The man was a trifle younger than Crowther, ginger-haired, snub-nosed and chunkily built. His name was Archie Fancourt. The woman's name was Bobbie Rogers. She was a blonde and apparently in the same profession as Miss Montague. She laughed a good deal; anything that anyone said which was the least bit amusing made Miss Roger's laugh. She had a fine set of teeth, which was perhaps why she liked opening her mouth.

These two were sitting in the back of an open Hispano-Suiza tourer, a gleaming monster of a car owned by Crowther. It was well known on the country roads in the vicinity of Braddlesham, where in the hands of its reckless owner it was looked upon as a considerable danger to life and limb.

Crowther introduced Debbie and Mark and opened a bottle of champagne. Mark felt out of his element, but he could see that Debbie was enjoying herself in this company. She was not in the least self-conscious, as he was, and he supposed that when you were in the habit of performing before the public you found no difficulty in mixing with any kind of society. But the more he became aware of her evident enjoyment the more marked became his own feeling of depression.

Crowther asked Debbie whether she had picked a horse for the next race, and she said she had.

'Mulligatawny. For a win.'

He gave a laugh. 'You'll be in the soup with that one. It's an old crocodile. Would you like to change your mind?'

'No; that's my choice and I'm sticking to it. Are you going to place the bets?'

'Yes,' Crowther said.

Debbie turned to Mark. 'Let me have two shillings for the stake.'

Mark took a florin from his pocket and handed it to her. She offered it to Crowther but he refused to take it.

'Keep your money. I'll put up the stakes for everyone. My treat.'

Debbie made no attempt to argue with him. She handed the coin back to Mark.

Crowther turned to him. 'Have you picked a horse?'

'I'm not betting,' Mark said. He preferred not to be indebted to Crowther. And he had seen the smiles on the faces of Fancourt and the two women when Debbie had mentioned two shillings as the stake. To them it probably seemed ridiculously small. In the company of these older people who lived in a different world from his he felt gauche and immature. He would have liked to walk away from the party, but he was afraid Debbie would not have come with him and he could not leave her.

Crowther shrugged. 'As you wish.'

He asked the others which horses they fancied and then went away to place the bets. Conversation flagged when he had gone. Debbie asked Archie Fancourt whether they were going back to London after the races.

'Oh, no,' he said. 'We're staying at Longmere.'

'London's so dreadfully hot at this time of year,' Miss Rogers said.

'Yes, I suppose it is,' Debbie said.

And that was that.

Crowther came back and a few minutes later the race started. By standing up in the car they were able to get a good view of the runners as they came round the final bend and into the finishing straight, and Crowther let Debbie use his binoculars. She made no effort to disguise her excitement when it became apparent that Mulligatawny was in the lead. Indeed, she gave vocal encouragement to horse and rider as they galloped towards the winning-post.

'Come on, Mulligatawny! Come on boy!'

The others in the party were less enchanted when they saw their own choices falling behind. There was a bunch of horses coming along the rails and the jockeys were using their whips; but it was apparent that Mulligatawny was still pulling away from the field and at the post he was a full two lengths clear.

Debbie was delighted, clapping her hands and laughing. 'How was that for an old crocodile?' she said to Crowther. 'Now admit you were wrong.'

'I was wrong,' Crowther said, 'and you were right. You must have been hanging round the stables.' He did not seem at all put out by this confounding of his own judgement; in fact he seemed almost as pleased as Debbie. 'I'll go and collect your winnings.'

When he returned he was carrying a

handful of five-pound notes. Mark had hardly ever seen one of those big white notes with the black lettering; occasionally one would be passed across the counter of the grocery shop and Mr Ringer would be very suspicious of it, thinking it might be a forgery. But it did not happen often.

Crowther counted out a batch of these notes and held them out to Debbie. 'There you are.'

She stared at the money. 'But this is far too much. The odds were ten to one. Ten times two shillings is only a pound.'

'Oh,' Crowther said, 'I put five pounds on. I never bet less than a fiver.'

'But I can't take all this.'

'Of course you can. It's yours.'

'Well,' she said, wavering, 'I suppose it is after all.' She took the money. 'Thank you. Thank you very much indeed.'

Mark reflected that she had not put up much resistance to accepting the winnings even though she had come by them in a rather questionable manner. He wished she had refused, but he could see that it would have been too much to expect.

She was counting the notes. When she had counted them she took one off the top and made a move to return it to Crowther.

'You've given me too much. You've included the stake money.'

'Of course. Didn't I tell you it was my treat? And besides, I owe you that for the tip. I put fifty on Mulligatawny for myself.' He still had a thick wad of notes in his hand and he held it up for her to see. 'These are my winnings.'

'But you said it was a crocodile.'

'I changed my mind. You persuaded me. You're a very clever girl.' He turned to Miss Montague for confirmation. 'Wouldn't you say Miss Layton is a clever girl, Lavinia?'

'I don't know about clever,' Miss Montague said, 'but she's certainly lucky.' She spoke sourly and the smile she gave was forced; it looked more like a sneer.

Mark could see that she resented the presence of the girl. She was probably jealous of the attention Crowther was paying to Debbie. Mark himself was not happy about it either; he did not like the way Crowther looked at her; it was the look of a man whose interest is aroused. There was calculation in it too, a weighing-up of chances perhaps. There could be no doubt that he was attracted; he was making no effort to disguise the fact. Mark was aware of it and Lavinia Montague was aware of it too. And neither of them liked it at all.

There were two more races. Debbie picked a horse in each of them and Crowther put money on them, but neither finished in the first three. He took the results with good humour.

'You can't expect to win every time, can you?'

Debbie was not bothered either. With Crowther still putting up the money for her bets it was costing her nothing, and at the end of the meeting she was fifty-five pounds to the good and in high spirits.

For her it had been a most successful day at the races.

11 Unhappy Ending

Crowther gave them a lift into town in the Hispano; there was plenty of room in it for six. He set them down not far from the Pier Pavilion and they watched him drive away. Mark was relieved to see the back of the car. He had been afraid that Crowther might invite them to join in some further diversions that would perhaps have gone on until late in the night. He had a feeling that Debbie would have accepted such an invitation.

'Well,' he said when the car had gone, 'that's that. I didn't imagine things were going to turn out the way they did.'

'Neither did I,' Debbie said. 'It was a marvellous piece of luck falling in with Hugh. It made the day.'

Mark was unhappy to hear her say that; it seemed to imply that until Crowther appeared on the scene she had not been having an enjoyable time. For him it had been the other way round; he had ceased to enjoy the afternoon from that moment forward.

'How did you come to know him?' he asked.

'Oh, it was quite by chance. It happened last autumn when we were performing at Heyworth. I'd been for a walk in the afternoon just to get away from the others for a time, and as a matter of fact I'd gone further than I meant to. He came along in that big car of his and offered to give me a lift.'

'Was he alone?'

'Yes, he was. But what has that got to

do with it?'

'Nothing. So you accepted the offer?'

'Well, why not? As I said, I'd gone further than I intended and it was a happy chance because I was tired of walking.'

'So that's how you became acquainted?'

'Yes. He told me who he was and I told him who I was. And that's all there is to it.'

She knew this was not the truth. There was more to it than that. There was for example the fact that before they reached Heyworth in the Hispano-Suiza Crowther asked her if she would like to take a look at his place, Longmere Hall, which was only a few miles away. She said she would. Well, it would have seemed churlish to refuse when he added that he would drive her back to Heyworth in good time for the evening performance. So they went to Longmere, and Crowther showed her round the place and was very polite and gentlemanly. And then he ordered afternoon tea for the two of them, which was brought to them by a manservant, very suave and well-mannered. After which he took her back to Heyworth as he had said he would

And that really was all. Except that he

turned up now and then at other places where The Merrymakers were performing and made himself known to her parents and rather ingratiated himself with them by telling them he thought their daughter had considerable talent and ought to go far. He even hinted that he might be able to be of some assistance in that respect, but he did not say how and none of them really expected anything to come of it.

All this she decided it might be wise not to reveal to Mark, because he seemed to be rather touchy on the subject of Hugh Crowther and might not understand.

'He's a bit of a bounder, you know.'

She stared at him. 'Now what makes you say that?'

'It's common knowledge in Braddlesham.'

'Oh, Braddlesham!' She sounded contemptuous. 'Village people are so narrow-minded.'

'Well, he's a drone, isn't he? Doesn't work for a living.'

'Why should he if he's rich enough not to have to? I suppose you think that's immoral?'

Mark made no reply to this. They were strolling along the promenade, mingling with the human tide. To their left the beach was becoming depopulated as the deckchairs and sand-castles were abandoned in favour of the evening entertainments. Soon, as daylight faded, the coloured lights would be coming on to give that bejewelled effect which was so great an attraction of the darker hours. But to Mark none of this was of so much interest as the girl at his side.

'I don't think you should have taken his money,' he said.

'Now what are you talking about?'

'You know what I'm talking about. Those Mulligatawny winnings.'

'Why on earth not? They were mine, weren't they?'

'But it was Mr Crowther who made the bet with his money.'

'Well, before we joined his party you were laying bets for me with your money.'

'That was different.'

'So what you're saying is that it would have been quite all right for me to take any winnings which might have come my way when you were putting up the stake, but not when Hugh Crowther was doing it. Is that it?'

'Well, yes.'

'Why?'

He felt himself being backed into a corner. If she could not appreciate the difference between his position and Crowther's in this matter, how could he explain it to her? It should have been so obvious that there would have been no need for an explanation. It all had to do with the kind of relationship that existed between them. So was he putting too high a rating on that relationship? Did it mean far less to her than it did to him?

Again he avoided giving a straight answer.

'You know he's taken with you, of course?'

'Now you really are talking rubbish.'

'Rubbish, is it? Didn't you see the way he kept looking at you? That woman, Lavinia Montague, noticed it. I could tell. He was supposed to be with her, but while you were there he hardly bothered to speak to her. He was giving all his attention to you. And she didn't like it.'

'You're imagining things,' she said. But she was not as emphatic about it as she might have been. 'He was simply being polite.'

'It was more than politeness. And I believe you knew it. It seemed to me you

133

liked it. You did nothing to discourage him.'

'Oh, really!' she said; and he could tell that she was becoming angry now. 'What was I supposed to do? Tell him not to speak to me? Not to look at me?'

'You could have refused to take his money.'

'So we're back to that, are we? Look here, Mark Ringer; what gives you the right to tell me what I ought or ought not to do? You don't own me, you know.'

'I'm not saying I do. All the same, I thought—'

Suddenly she turned on him. 'I'm getting fed up with you, and I don't give a bloody damn what you thought. Understand? Not a bloody sodding damn.'

He was taken aback by this outburst, which was shrill enough to cause a few people to turn their heads and stare. It was the language that really shook him. He had never heard her swear before and he would not have imagined her capable of speaking like that. He supposed it was the way she had been brought up. Perhaps in the kind of company she kept such expletives were commonplace. But it pained him to hear them coming from her lips.

He said nothing. It was as though he had been struck dumb by the virulence of her attack and could find no answer to it. She too was silent for a while, and they walked on, still side by side but not speaking.

Then she said: 'I'm sorry, Mark. I shouldn't have gone off the deep end like that.'

'It's all right,' he said. 'It doesn't matter.'

But it did.

'It's just that you—well, sometimes you can be so righteous. And I can't keep up with it, that's all. I'm the way I am. And that's how you'll have to take me. I can't change.'

'I don't want you to.'

Only in some ways, he thought, only in some ways. But whether she changed or not, it would make no difference to the way he felt about her. He could not help loving her, whatever blemishes might be revealed.

She was not sitting on the usual bench when he went to look for her the next morning. They had made no arrangement for a meeting when they had parted the previous day, but it had become a regular thing and he was disappointed not to find her there. So perhaps she had really meant it when she had said she was fed up with him; perhaps she did not wish to see him again.

And then a thought came into his head: she had money now, quite a lot of it, so maybe she no longer needed him to pay for things. It was not a pleasant thought and he tried to dismiss it from his mind, because it sullied the whole of their relationship, turning it into something hollow and mercenary—on her part at least.

But still it persisted. Nagging.

He hung around for some time. He walked up and down the promenade, returning to the bench again and again. But she was still not there and he had to accept the fact that she was not coming.

He blamed Crowther; it was all because of him. If it had not been for that chance encounter at the races all would still have been well. So why did it have to happen? Why did Crowther have to choose that particular day to take his party to those particular races? It was fate, an evil fate that had ruined everything.

He gave up and went away. It was all over between him and Debbie; he might as well accept this painful fact. He had never really meant anything to her and now she had finished with him. He had been a fool to expect anything else.

But hope returned with the afternoon. He went again to the bench and she was there.

'Oh,' she said, 'there you are. I'd begun to think you weren't coming.'

'I came this morning. I waited and waited, but you didn't turn up.'

'I had other things to do.' She spoke coldly. He got the impression that meeting him was of less importance to her than a host of other things.

He sat down beside her with a sense of awkwardness because of the way they had parted the previous day, on that rather sour note. He could not forget what she had said to him then, and he wondered whether it was in her mind also.

There was a small brown-paper parcel resting on the bench on the other side of her. She picked it up and handed it to him.

'This is for you.'

He held it in his hand and looked at it,

and then at her, surprised, tongue-tied.

'Well,' she said, 'aren't you going to see what it is?'

'Yes, of course.'

He tore the brown-paper wrapping off and revealed a morocco-bound book with gold lettering on the cover. It was Palgrave's anthology of poetry, *The Golden Treasury*.

'Look inside,' she said.

He opened the book and on the flyleaf he read; 'To Mark from D. With love.'

'Oh, Debbie!' he said. 'Oh, Debbie!'

'It's by way of a peace offering. You told me you liked poetry, so I thought this would be just the thing to give you.'

There was no suggestion of a chill in her voice now; it was warm and intimate.

'Oh, Debbie!' he said again. 'Thank you.'

It occurred to him that one of those other things she had had to do that morning had been to hunt in the bookshops for this gift. How badly he had misjudged her! It made him remorseful.

She was smiling at him, bewitchingly. 'Friends again?'

'More than friends,' he said.

Oh, so much more than that!

On the last day of his holiday he gave her a present. It was a lucky charm in the shape of a tiny black cat suspended on a thin gold chain. It had taken almost all the money he had left to buy it.

'Thank you, Mark,' she said. 'It's nice. It's very nice.'

But she did not go into raptures about it, and he could not help being rather disappointed.

'You like it?'

'Why, of course I like it. It was sweet of you to get it for me.'

Which would have been all very well if he had not been hoping for something a trifle more demonstrative. But perhaps he was being over-sensitive in detecting a certain lack of enthusiasm in her acceptance of his gift. Perhaps. Yet he could not avoid the feeling that if it had been of greater value she might have received it with considerably stronger evidence of pleasure.

The final parting was somewhat low-key also.

'When shall I see you again?' he asked.

She shrugged. 'I don't know. We shall be here for a few more weeks, but I expect I'll be working again.'

'I doubt whether I could have managed to get over here anyway.' He would have had a lot of explaining to do, and where would he have found the money? He could hardly ask his father to fork out again just yet.

'Well, then,' she said, 'I suppose it'll have to wait until we visit Braddlesham in the autumn.'

He was depressed by the offhand way in which she said it. It did not appear to bother her that they would have to wait so long before they could meet again. And even then it would be difficult to arrange things so that they had much time together on their own. Braddlesham was a different kind of place from this.

'I shall miss you horribly,' he said. 'I just don't know what I'll do without you.'

'You'll manage. It's not the end of the world, you know.'

He noticed that she did not say she would miss him. Perhaps she knew she would not. Perhaps when he was gone he would slip entirely out of her mind. Even in their farewell kiss there was a notable lack of passion—on her part at least. Perhaps it's all over, he thought. Perhaps it's been nothing to her but a passing fancy, something to fill in the time when she was not working. Perhaps she never really wants to see me again.

It was a wretched thought to carry away with him from a holiday which had seemed at times to offer so much but in the end had become less than satisfactory. For him, if not for her, the ending had been an unhappy one.

12 Moves in the Game

At the weekend Hugh Crowther abruptly broke up his house-party at Longmere Hall and sent the guests on their way. The only explanation he gave for this sudden decision was that something had cropped up.

Archie Fancourt took the news without complaint and little surprise; he had been acquainted with Crowther and his whims long enough to know that he was completely unpredictable and studied nobody's interests but his own. The women were less phlegmatic concerning this unexpected termination of a pleasant holiday, and Lavinia Montague was particularly upset; especially when she discovered that she was not even going to be transported back to London in the Hispano-Suiza but had to be content with a back seat in Fancourt's far less sumptuous Riley.

'That,' she said, 'is about all you could expect from a rich bastard like Hugh Crowther.'

But this remark was made in private to Miss Bobbie Rogers, because she had no desire to antagonize a rich bastard who might have other treats to offer in the future. And he had, after all, given her a few trifles of jewellery, so she was not going away entirely empty-handed.

With the guests safely out of the way, Crowther was free on the Monday morning to make a trip to the seaside, where he was able to have a heart-to-heart talk with the Laytons.

The interview took place in the sitting-room of the house where the family had taken digs for the summer season. It was a small dim room with more worn armchairs than could reasonably have been expected to be packed into such a confined space. Fortunately, at this particular time there

142

was no one occupying the chairs except Howard Layton, his wife Gloria and Hugh Crowther, and they were able to have their discussion in complete privacy.

Crowther, without any beating about the bush, got down immediately to the subject that he had in mind.

'I've been thinking over what you told me some time ago regarding the hopes you have for your daughter's career on the stage.'

'Ah!' Layton said.

Gloria said nothing, but he could see that she was giving him all her attention. This was a subject dear to the hearts of both of them.

'I believe I suggested then, if you remember, that I might possibly be able to give some help in that line.'

'Why, yes,' Layton said. 'I think you did mention something of the sort.'

He remembered very clearly. He had discussed the matter with his wife and they had agreed rather sadly that it would be unwise to hope for much to come from something as vague as that. It was the kind of thing people said for effect. And having heard nothing from Crowther in the months that had passed since then, they had reluctantly come to the conclusion that his half-promise had indeed been nothing more than empty words. But now here the man was once again bringing up the subject. So perhaps—

'I don't know whether I told you that I have certain connections with the theatre?'

'I don't think you did,' Layton said.

'No? Well, I have.'

He had in fact put money into a musical comedy called *Follow That Star*. He had at the time been very much attracted to an actress named Sophia Morton, who was to be the leading lady, and it was she who had persuaded him to become a backer; otherwise known as an angel. The show was a flop and was taken off at the end of the first week. Crowther lost his money and Sophia too, but he retained a number of show business acquaintances and still hung on to the fringes of the theatre world, where he was quite well-known and could pick up some desirable female company such as Lavinia Montague and Bobbie Rogers whenever he felt so inclined.

'Now,' Crowther said, 'the point is this. We know very well that Debbie has talent, but to really get ahead she needs to be where the action is. London.'

'That's exactly what Howard and I have always said,' Gloria remarked. 'She needs to be noticed by the right people.'

'I could introduce her to the right people.'

'You would be prepared to do that, Mr Crowther?'

'It would be a pleasure.'

'But hold on a minute,' Layton said. 'She isn't in London.'

'She could be.'

'Oh, I don't know—'

'You're thinking about the expense, of course,' Crowther said. 'But it wouldn't cost much. I know an excellent woman who has a boarding-house in Bloomsbury. Her name is Mrs Mason and she used to be housekeeper for an uncle of mine who died some years ago. With the help of a bit of money he left her she decided to set up in business on her own account. I know her well, a most respectable lady, I assure you. Now if you're agreeable, and Debbie is too of course, I could arrange for her to lodge at the Bloomsbury house at a very reasonable charge, and I'm sure Mrs Mason would keep a motherly eye on her. You wouldn't need to worry about her at all.'

'Well,' Mrs Layton said, 'that sounds all right.' But she still seemed to have some doubts. 'She's very young, of course. Only eighteen.'

'In her profession you need to start young. If you haven't reached the top by the time you're twenty-five or so you're never likely to make it. But who am I to be telling you? You know the score better than I do.'

He smiled at Gloria, and she had to admit that he was a charming man. Not exactly young, of course, but young enough. In the prime of life. And a man of the world who knew his way around. But was he to be trusted?

Crowther did not stay very long. He knew better than to press the idea too hard. Having planted the seed, he knew that it could safely be left to germinate and grow without his help.

'Think about it,' he said. 'Talk it over with Debbie. I'll call in again tomorrow to hear what you've decided.'

He went away without even seeing the girl. That was calculated too. Everything he did was calculated.

'He's not offering to do this out of the

goodness of his heart, you know,' Layton said, after Crowther had departed. 'People aren't made like that except in books by Charles Dickens. Deb has caught his eye; that's the long and the short of it.'

'But Howard, he's far too old for her.'

'He may not think so. Not much over thirty, I'd imagine.'

'So you think we ought not to let her go?'

'I'd be happier if we were going with her. To keep an eye on things.'

'But that's impossible. We can't break this engagement at the Pavilion. And even if we could, we need the money.'

'I know.'

Mrs Layton was silent for a while. She appeared to be studying a particularly repulsive framed oleograph hanging above the mantelpiece, but she was not really seeing it because her mind was so fully occupied with the decision that had to be made.

'She should be all right, don't you think? It's not as if she'll be staying with Mr Crowther in his London house. She'll be at that Mrs Mason's boarding-house. She'll only be with him during the day. Nothing can happen.'

Howard Layton knew what she meant when she said nothing could happen. He also knew that she was simply trying to convince herself of this. It was such a difficult choice to make. Did they take this risk with their adored daughter or did they deny her a golden opportunity to get her foot on the ladder to fame and fortune? The thing was as clear-cut as that.

And in the end it was Debbie herself who made the decision. As it had been bound to be. Made in an instant, with never a moment's pause for consideration.

'Of course I must go. It's just the chance I've been waiting for. You can't stop me now. You can't.'

And of course they could not.

Crowther came again the next morning, and they told him they had decided to accept his kind offer. He gave an enigmatic smile. He had expected nothing less.

Debbie, who was present on this occasion, added her thanks to those of her parents. 'It's so good of you, Hugh. Thank you. Thank you ever so.'

A startled glance passed between the father and mother. They had not imagined that their daughter was on Christian name terms with Crowther. The glance seemed to say: 'Are we doing the right thing?' But it was too late to have second thoughts now. The die had been cast.

'The question now,' Crowther said, 'is when can you leave? I suggest the sooner the better. No point in wasting time. How about tomorrow afternoon? Can you be ready by then?'

Debbie answered quickly: 'Yes.'

'Good. I'll get on the phone to Mrs Mason and arrange about the room. And I'll call for you tomorrow at three.'

'I'll be ready,' Debbie said.

Howard and Gloria Layton said nothing. They seemed to be bewildered by the speed with which things were moving. It was as if everything had now been taken out of their hands and they had no more power to control events.

Crowther arrived in the Hispano-Suiza promptly at the time arranged. Debbie had her luggage packed and was waiting for him. Her farewells to her parents did not take long; a hug and a kiss for each of them, and then she was getting into the car.

Crowther gave a parting wave of the hand to the older Laytons, standing rather forlornly on the pavement.

'So long.'

They made no reply, just stood there silently watching as he started his gleaming chariot and drove away. Debbie did not even look back.

It was a distance of rather more than a hundred miles to London and she enjoyed every yard of it. It was not the first time she had travelled in this beautiful car, but this was by far the longest journey she had made in it. The weather was fine and the hood was down, and when Crowther really put his foot on the accelerator the car seemed to surge forward like a mettlesome horse that had been given the spur. She could hear the drumming of the tyres on the road and the wind tore at them with invisible fingers, and it was even more exhilarating than sweeping down the steepest parts of the Scenic Railway.

They reached London late in the afternoon and drove straight to the Bloomsbury boarding-house where Debbie was to stay. It was in a quiet street not far from the British Museum, and it was just one of a row of similar houses that looked as if they had been gently weathering for at least a century.

Mrs Mason turned out to be a middle-aged grey-haired woman wearing gold-rimmed spectacles. She was thin and bony and had on a dress of some stiff black material, which rustled softly when she moved and was buttoned up to the neck. She spoke respectfully to Crowther and addressed him as Mr Hugh.

'You can depend on me to do my best to make the young lady comfortable while she is under my roof,' she said.

Crowther smiled at her. 'I'm sure I can, Mrs Mason. I know of no one more dependable than you.'

The room was on the second floor and was reached by means of a broad staircase which spiralled its way up from the tiled entrance hall to the landings above. It was not a large room, but it was not cramped either. The furnishings were plain but adequate.

'You was lucky, Mr Hugh,' Mrs Mason said. 'Fell vacant only last week.'

'Business is good, then?'

'Can't grumble, sir. Considering.'

Crowther did not stay long. He said he

would leave Debbie to get settled in while he went off to install himself in his own house, which was in fact not too far away in Belgravia. He suggested that if Debbie were agreeable they might go to a theatre in the evening; in which case he would call for her later.

She thought it was a delightful idea. She had never in her life been to a West End theatre, but she did not tell him so. She wished to appear as sophisticated and experienced as possible in the company of this rich and knowledgeable man of the world.

'That would be lovely.'

'It's settled then. Fine.'

He left her in the room and went downstairs with Mrs Mason, with whom he talked for a few minutes in the hall. Money changed hands, and then he left the house and got into the Hispano. As he drove away there was an exultant smile on his face. So far things were going very satisfactorily; very satisfactorily indeed. All the moves in the game had been made exactly according to plan and he looked forward to succeeding moves being equally successful. He was so pleased with himself that he hummed a snatch of tune. Really, there was nothing like being a rich man without the necessity of sordid toil. It gave you so much freedom of movement. And so much power.

13 Where Else?

He called for her, not in the Hispano but in a taxi. It was, he said, more convenient when you were going out for the evening.

'You don't have the bother of finding a place to park the thing.'

This again was a new experience for Debbie, and she was thrilled. In her mind there had always been a certain aura of romance about the London taxicab; it was so different from other forms of transport. Not that there was anything particularly romantic about its appearance; it was just a little black box on wheels. But perhaps it was this very ordinariness that gave it its charm. And then, to be riding in one set you apart from *hoi polloi* who thronged the pavements or travelled in buses or tube trains. Once she had made her way up the ladder of her profession she would always travel around London by taxi. How marvellous it would be!

She was enchanted by the lights, the glitter of the shop fronts, the teeming life of the streets; the entire metropolis seemed to be in motion. Where were all these people going? Did they even know?

'Enjoying it?' Crowther asked.

'Oh, yes. It's so exciting, isn't it?'

They had dinner in an Italian restaurant in Soho. She was hungry and did full justice to the meal. Crowther seemed amused.

'You have the appetite of youth,' he said.

She was somewhat abashed. Perhaps she had strayed beyond the limit of good manners by eating so voraciously. Would it have been more ladylike merely to peck at the food? She reflected sadly that you did not learn all there was to know about the way to behave in good society by travelling around with a third-rate troupe of entertainers. For them a supper of kippers was a treat, or fish and chips, sprinkled with salt and vinegar and eaten with the fingers out of a week-old newspaper.

They went to the Aldwych Theatre

where the regular company of Ralph Lynn, Tom Walls, Robertson Hare and the rest was appearing in a Ben Travers farce. Somehow or other Crowther had obtained tickets; she did not know how; and the seats were in an excellent position. The play was tremendously funny; she could not remember ever having laughed so much. And how well the players knew how to put it across! They were true professionals. Such timing, such superbly executed business, such overall expertise! When she compared this with the short sketches put on by The Merrymakers it made her cringe.

Before leaving her at Mrs Mason's Crowther said he would call again in the morning and they would get down to business. She thanked him for a delightful evening and he said she was not to give it a thought; he had enjoyed it himself.

When he had gone she reflected that there had been only one fly in the ointment: it was that her clothes had not been equal to the occasion. The dress she had worn was well past its best, and it had been cheap and shoddy even when new. Crowther had been wearing a dark blue suit which bore the stamp of high-class tailoring and she felt that she had rather let him down. But what could she have done about it when her wardrobe was so limited? She suspected that even the blue suit had been worn in order not to make her feel uncomfortable and that otherwise he might have been in evening-dress.

As if to confirm her misgivings concerning her wardrobe, the first thing Crowther did next day was to take her on a shopping expedition in the West End.

'You must have some decent things to wear if you're going to impress people.'

'But won't that be horribly expensive?'

'Leave me to worry about that. It will cost you nothing.'

'But I can't let you—'

'You can't stop me,' he said. 'Now don't be obstinate, there's a good girl. I am doing all this to please myself, so you don't need to feel the least bit guilty in accepting things from me.'

If fact she had no intention of being obstinate; she simply thought she ought to make a show of reluctance for form's sake. If, as he said, he was doing it all to please himself, why should she object? The money probably meant nothing to him anyway.

So they ventured into the fashionable shops of Regent Street and Piccadilly, where Crowther proved himself a very shrewd adviser in the matter of women's clothes and quite capable of holding his own in any argument with snooty saleswomen. Indeed, he seemed to get as much enjoyment from the operation as Debbie herself, who was overwhelmed by the riches of outerwear and underwear that were showered upon her.

At the end she had no idea how much it had all cost and she did not enquire. Crowther bought a suitcase to hold most of the things and they had lunch in a restaurant before returning to the Bloomsbury boarding-house. Here he told Debbie to get into one of the new outfits because they were going to see a man who might be useful to her and it was essential to make a favourable impression on him.

When she saw the man she was not sure whether or not he was favourably impressed by her but she was dead certain she was not by him. His name was Cowan.

They found him in a stuffy little office in a narrow street off Shaftesbury Avenue. The office was up two flights of uncarpeted stairs a steep as a ladder. It looked like a dumping-place for wastepaper; on the walls were playbills and there were shelves sagging under loose-leaf files. Cowan was sitting at a kneehole desk on which was a telephone and more of the paper. There was another desk on the opposite side of the room with a typewriter on it. A scraggy woman with a sharp nose, a tangled mass of hair and a string of beads dangling from her neck was seated at this desk and pecking at the typewriter with fingers tipped with blood-red nails.

'Oi, oi!' Cowan said as Crowther walked in with Debbbie. 'So you got here.'

He was short and fat and bald and greasy. He was wearing a pair of baggy trousers supported by elastic braces and a blue-and-white striped shirt with sweat stains under the armpits. On his feet were scuffed suede shoes and stuck in the side of his mouth was a half-smoked cigar which stayed there when he spoke. The office was filled with the aroma of the smoke.

'Yes, we got here,' Crowther said. 'It wasn't too difficult apart from the stairs.'

Cowan grinned. 'Them stairs! Oi, oi!'

There was no spare chair, so Crowther pushed some of the papers aside and sat on Cowan's desk, at his ease, one leg swinging.

Cowan looked at Debbbie. 'This is the young lady that's looking for fame and fortune in showbiz, is it?'

'Yes.'

'It's a tough profession, love. You know that?'

'I know it,' Debbie said.

'You gotta work hard and fight like hell. And then you may not make it. Even with talent and looks you may not make it. You gotta have luck as well. Are you lucky?'

'I don't know,' Debbie said. She had taken an instant dislike to Cowan and the dislike was growing by the minute. She was repelled by his appearance and she could smell his body odour in spite of the cigar smoke.

Crowther had taken a gold cigarette-case from his pocket and was lighting a cigarette with a gold lighter. The contrast between his elegance and Cowan's slovenliness could not have been more marked.

'Dance and sing, do you?' Cowan asked.

'Yes.'

'She's good,' Crowther said. 'I've seen her perform.'

Cowan ignored him. 'Let's see your legs, sweetheart.'

Debbie hesitated. The hem of the skirt she was wearing came just below the knee and that was where she would have liked it to remain. She had never been at all shy of revealing her legs on stage, but somehow she felt reluctant to exhibit them to this gross oily man with his little piggy eyes. The woman with the beads had stopped pecking at the keys of the typewriter and was looking at her.

'Come on, girl,' Cowan said. 'Don't be bashful. We're all grown-up people here and we've seen a pair of female pins before now. Lift your skirt and let's have a butcher's.'

She reached down and raised the hem of the skirt above her knees.

'Higher,' Cowan said.

She lifted the skirt above her thighs and felt soiled by Cowan's gaze. It seemed lecherous to her.

'Not bad,' he said. 'Not bad at all. Mind you, it takes more than a good pair of legs and a pretty face and a nice figure. But they do help. You ain't got them and where are you? Nowhere. Might as well go home and take up knitting.'

160

When they had left Cowan's office and were walking away in the direction of Shaftesbury Avenue Crowther said:

'He was impressed. No doubt about that.'

'It didn't seem like that to me,' Debbie said.

'Possibly not. He keeps his cards close to his chest, doesn't give much away. But I've known him a long time and I can tell when someone's making an impression on him. And you were.'

'Do you think he can help?'

'He knows a lot of people and he has influence. He's got your name and he won't just sit on it. You do believe me, don't you?'

'Well, yes,' she said. 'Yes, of course I do.' But somehow she could not see that fat slob with the chewed-down cigar in the corner of his mouth doing much for her. It just did not seem likely.

There was no more business that day. They strolled around for a while, looked at the playbills outside the theatres, did some window-shopping, breathed in the exhaust fumes from the motor vehicles and had afternoon tea in a bijou tea-shop.

'Tonight,' Crowther said, 'we are having a party.'

'Are we?' It was the first she had heard about it. Yet he must have had it all arranged. 'Where?'

'At my place, of course. Where else?'

Where else indeed!

14 Closed Chapter

It was not a big party. Archie Fancourt was there but not Lavinia Montague or Bobbie Rogers. Fancourt was escorting a blonde named Marilyn Morgan.

He looked at Debbie with a knowing grin when he introduced her to the blonde.

'Miss Layton is a racing tipster.'

Debbie was not sure whether Miss Morgan believed this or was only pretending to.

'How utterly marvellous! Do you go around shouting "I gotta horse!"?'

'No,' Debbie said. 'He's telling lies.'

'He always does. It's so naughty.'

'What happened to that boy you were with?' Fancourt asked. 'Mark something.'

162

'He went home. What happened to that woman you were with? Bobbie something.'

Archie Fancourt reddened and laughed and edged away, taking the blonde with him. She seemed to be questioning him about something.

There were a few other couples and she assumed they were all friends of Crowther's. It was the first time she had been to his town house and she could see that it was not nearly as large as Longmere Hall. It was certainly not small, however; the rooms had high decorated ceilings and were sumptuously furnished. Heavy velvet curtains hung in rich folds at the windows and there were many *objets d'art*, for he would have sudden urges to collect such things, though he had no dedication to this pursuit.

The house was staffed by a manservant and his wife, who acted as cook and housekeeper, and a couple of maids. They were not overworked, since Crowther was away from the house for more time than he was in it, and it was probable that they had ways of adding to the wages he paid them.

The party went well. There was an unlimited supply of alcoholic drinks and a buffet from which the guests could help themselves when they felt the need for food. A Marconi self-changing radiogram with a plentiful supply of records provided music for dancing, and Crowther danced a lot with Debbie. She thought he danced very well but held her a little too closely. She also thought the act of holding her excited him, but she was not altogether surprised at this. Young as she was, she knew the kind of effect she had on men.

Nor was she greatly surprised when she woke in the morning to find herself in bed with him. This, of course, was what it had all been leading up to; this was why he had been so willing to give his help in the advancement of her career. He wanted her.

Well, it was fair enough; you had to pay for everything in this wicked world; that was the way it worked. Nothing was for nothing. What was that American saying? There's no such thing as a free lunch. So her lunch was not to be free; nor all the other meals; nor the new clothes; nor the taxi rides. All right then; so be it. Just so long as he fulfilled his side of the bargain it was fine as far as she was concerned.

It was a pity about the hangover, though. She had a throbbing ache in the head and her tongue felt like a strip of old shoe leather.

She had only the haziest memory of the latter part of the previous evening. She had drunk too much; champagne and other stuff. Crowther had encouraged her to do it; and things had become fuzzy, blurred round the edges. She had had an impression that people were leaving, just drifting away. And then Crowther was leading her to the bedroom; though leading was not quite the word because his arm was round her and he was in fact more or less carrying her; her legs having given up working. After that he was helping her to undress and lifting her into bed. Then he was getting in beside her. And then...

She became aware that he was also awake and watching her, perhaps with a shade of amusement.

She said: 'You seduced me, didn't you?'

The amusement turned to laughter. 'Is that what you call it? As I recall, you didn't raise any objection.'

'I was squiffy, that's why.'

'And if you hadn't been squiffy, would it have made any difference?'

She made no answer to that. She just said: 'You had this in mind all along, didn't you?'

He did not bother to deny it. 'Of course.'

'Why?'

'Why! My dear girl, do you have to ask such a question? Because you are so enchanting, so utterly ravishing. You've bewitched me. That's the plain truth of the matter.'

She was silent. She felt flattered, even though she told herself that this was probably just what he intended. Perhaps he was telling the truth; and it was not as if he did not have a wide choice: women like Lavinia Montague for example. Yet he had gone to considerable trouble in order to ensnare her, so he must really have been attracted.

'A penny for your thoughts,' he said.

She shook her head. 'That would be far too small a price.' And then: 'What do we do today?'

'First we go and fetch the rest of your things from Mrs Mason's.'

'You mean I'm moving in here?'

'It seems to me that you already have.'

'What will Mrs Mason say?'

'Nothing.'

'She'll be losing a lodger.'

'She won't shed any tears over that, believe me.'

'I suppose she knew what was happening from the start?'

'Does it matter?'

'No, it doesn't matter.'

She had to admit that she was having the time of her life. Crowther took her here, there and everywhere; sightseeing, theatre-going, the lot. And of course he was paying for everything; it was not costing her a brass farthing.

Her only regret was that nothing seemed to be moving in the matter of her theatrical advancement. It was true that she had had an audition, of sorts. According to Crowther, Cowan had arranged it for her, and it had taken place in a large, rather bare room with a stage at one end.

There were several other girls taking part, all somewhat casually dressed, and a man named Brian appeared to be in charge of the proceedings. He looked quite young until you got close to him, and then the lines on his face became apparent and you could tell he had been around for some considerable time. He was sitting at a plain deal table and smoking one cigarette after another. Sitting beside him was a woman with a face as plain as the table, who was making notes on a scribbling-pad and calling out the girls' names as their turns came to get up on the stage and show what they could do. A sad-looking man in a blue waistcoat and shirt-sleeves was rattling the keys on an upright piano when called upon to do so, apparently bored with the whole proceeding and just wanting to sneak away to the nearest pub.

When Debbie's turn came round she climbed on to the stage and did a bit of dancing and a bit of singing to the accompaniment of the piano, and that was that. The woman told her they would let her know.

'Don't call us. We'll call you.'

She knew that one. It was a showbiz cliché.

Nobody had even told her what show they were auditioning for. She asked Crowther when they were leaving. He had been sitting at the back, smoking, waiting for the business to be concluded. His answer seemed rather less than satisfactory to her.

168

'I don't think it's got very far yet. They're still looking for backers, so I hear.'

'But it is a musical?'

'Oh, yes.'

'Does it have a title?'

'Not yet.'

'It all sounds horribly vague to me.'

'Well, as I said, it's all up in the air at the moment. They're feeling their way.'

'Are you putting money into it?'

'I'm not sure. I haven't made up my mind.'

She was not very happy about it. Perhaps the only reason why they had given her an audition was that Crowther had asked them to and they wanted to be nice to him because they were hoping he would be an angel. She doubted whether anything would come of it.

Towards the end of the week she had a letter from her mother, forwarded from Mrs Mason's Bloomsbury boarding-house. Mrs Layton hoped things were going well and that Mrs Mason was looking after her. She detected a note of anxiety in the letter, though nothing was stated. Her father sent his love and they both looked forward to her return. They missed her.

She bought a picture postcard—Piccadilly Circus by night—and sent it to them. She was fine, she wrote. Things were moving. She loved London. Mrs Mason was a jewel. She hoped they were both well.

She had not given them a thought since she had been away.

The whole thing came to an end after a fortnight. Crowther said he thought it was time she went back to her parents; for the present there was no more to be done in London. She would hear as soon as anything turned up.

The fact was that he wanted to be rid of her. It was his way: a woman would catch his eye; he would be strongly attracted and would do everything in his power to obtain her. Then all would be marvellous for a time; he would do anything for her, spend money lavishly, assure her that he loved her to distraction. But the passion never lasted; he would tire of her and the affair would be finished; sometimes with tears and tantrums and bitter recriminations; but finished nevertheless.

Then someone else would come along and the drama would be run through again.

With Debbie Layton it had been a briefer infatuation than usual; perhaps because of her immaturity. She was, after all, little more than a child, and the youthful charms that at first had captivated him quickly began to pall. Moreover, she was forever plaguing him with demands that he should do more in the matter of this ridiculous ambition of hers to become a star of the London stage. He had no belief in it, but he did not tell her so. He had used it simply as a means to an end: the gratification of his own desire. And now that this object had been achieved he had no more interest in the business.

He was pleasantly surprised by the lack of any sharp reaction on her part when he told her that the affair was finished; for that was what in effect he was saying. She took it very calmly; no tears, no tantrums. The truth of the matter was that she was not reluctant to call it a day. On her side there had never been any great emotion involved in the brief relationship; indeed, simply as a lover she much preferred Mark Ringer. Ah, if only Mark had had money in sufficient quantity!

'You will be taking me back, I suppose?'
'Naturally.'

It was the least he could do.

When Crowther returned her to her parents he did not linger. He excused himself by saying that he was in rather a hurry to get back to Longmere. He climbed into the Hispano-Suiza and drove away without a backward glance. Another episode in his life had reached its inevitable conclusion. Or so he supposed.

Mrs Layton looked at the extra luggage that her daughter had brought back from London; the new suitcase and the new clothes she was wearing; and Debbie thought she was going to ask questions on the subject, but she merely pursed her lips and made no remark on these unexpected acquisitions. Perhaps she thought it advisable not to inquire too deeply into certain aspects of the London visit.

The summer season was drawing towards a close, and it was decided that Debbie should not return to the Pier Pavilion show for the few remaining weeks. When The Merrymakers took to the road in the autumn she would of course again be a star member of the troupe. That was if nothing turned up to alter the arrangement.

For a time the Laytons remained in a state of daily expectation that something would turn up; that there would be a letter or a telegram summoning Debbie immediately to London. But nothing came and hope faded. It was Gloria Layton who first put into words what both she and her husband had long been thinking.

'That man,' she said, 'was a fraud and an imposter.'

Howard Layton gave a sigh. 'My dear, I think you are right.'

It was just one more disappointment in a life that seemed to be full of them.

They made no mention to Debbie of their doubts concerning Hugh Crowther, and she never mentioned his name. It was as though they had all become resolved to regard that chapter as closed.

15 Bad Start

Howard Layton was not at all sorry to leave Heyworth. There had been that piece of bother with Dickie Wilson and the Drings and the manager of The Anchor, which had rather soured things for a time; and the audiences had been so poor in the Oddfellows Hall that there had been very little profit at the end of the run.

In addition a certain abrasiveness seemed to have entered into the relationship between Jackie Vernon and Maudie Maxted. They had always been such close friends; well, even more than that really; but now they tended to snap at each other over the merest trifle. Jackie was the one who usually started it; she would criticize Maudie, making biting remarks about her appearance or her performance or maybe just the way she did her hair or the shade of lipstick she used. Maudie would take it quietly for a while, but in the end she would flare up and answer back, trading insult for insult.

Layton wondered what had gone wrong between them. But it was not something he thought it advisable to delve into. It bothered him nevertheless; it was just one more worry, and he had enough of them as it was.

They moved on to Braddlesham on the Sunday and installed themselves at the Queen's Head, where Mr and Mrs

Simmonds were delighted to welcome them.

'We always look forward to having you and your people here, Mr Layton,' Mrs Simmonds said. 'As I say to Tom, it's not often we get to mix with theatre folk. Makes a nice change from what we get round here.'

'Gratified, madam,' Layton said. 'Highly gratified.'

He wondered how welcome they would be at the inn if the day ever came when he was unable to pay the bill for the accommodation. But he tried not to think about that because it only made him feel depressed.

'They've arrived,' Mr Ringer said as he carved the Sunday joint. 'I saw them as I was passing the Queen's Head.'

'They?' Mrs Ringer said.

'You know. The concert party. Merrymakers. They'll be putting up there as per usual.'

Angela sniffed. 'How exciting, I don't think.'

'Now, my girl, don't go looking down your nose again. They'll bring a bit of life into the place.'

Mark said nothing. It seemed amazing to him that no one else in the family realized that the Laytons and others of the troupe had been performing at the Pier Pavilion in the summer. He was glad that his mother and Angela had not been to the show; otherwise they would have been bound to recognize some of The Merrymakers in the company. Not that they would necessarily have deduced from this that he was meeting Debbie every day; but they might have had suspicions; especially Angela; you could trust her to nose things out.

He had kept the photograph of him and Debbie safely hidden away, but he had not been so careful with *The Golden Treasury* and his mother had picked it up and read the inscription. Naturally she had wanted to know who had given it to him.

Driven into a corner, all he could think of to say was the truth. 'That girl.'

'You mean the one you took to your room at Aunt Alice's?'

'Yes.'

'But this is signed "D". I thought you said her name was Louise.'

'No. Diana.'

'I feel quite sure you said Louise.'

176

'Well, I may have. It's her second name. Diana Louise Johnson, that's what she is. But she told me to call her Louise because she liked it better than Diana.'

'If that's the case I'd have thought she would have signed herself "L".' Mrs Ringer sounded suspicious. 'I hope you're telling the truth, Mark.'

'Of course I am. Why shouldn't I?'

'Do you write to her?'

'No. I couldn't even if I wanted to. I don't know her address.'

'It seems very odd to me. She gives you a present like this—with love—and you don't even exchange addresses so you can keep in touch.'

'Well, that's the way it is.'

'Did you give her anything?'

'Yes. A lucky charm. Nothing much.'

'I still think it's a great pity,' Mrs Ringer said, 'that you didn't introduce her to me. It was very thoughtless of you.'

'It wouldn't have helped.'

She gave him a long hard look. 'Sometimes, Mark, I just don't understand you; really I don't.'

He had thought of going over to Heyworth while The Merrymakers were appearing there, but he had been unable to pluck up the courage. Though he longed to see Debbie again and talk to her, he was apprehensive. Weeks, months even, had passed since that fortnight at the seaside, and he had lost touch with her altogether. How could he be sure that she even wanted to see him again?

So he had not gone to Heyworth; instead he had waited for the troupe to come to Braddlesham. And now they were here. Debbbie was no further away from him than the Queen's Head, which was scarcely half a minute's walk from Alfred Ringer's grocery shop. If he wished he could go there and ask to speak to Miss Deborah Layton; it was as simple as that. But he knew he would not do it. Even if he could have masterd his own shyness, he had to consider her feelings. He felt certain she would not have wanted him to do it. She might have been very angry with him, and what good would have come of it then? No; somehow he had to contrive to meet her in private. But he could not see how to arrange it.

'How's that for you, Mark?' Mr Ringer asked, forking a slice of beef on to his plate. 'You'd like some fat to go with it,

I expect. Look as if you could do with some fatting up. Getting quite peaky you are these days. Haven't fallen in love again, have you?'

Angela giggled and Mark felt himself going hot in the face and was angry because he could not control the flush. He mumbled something about his father talking rubbish and made a not very successful effort to appear nonchalant.

'Perhaps you're studying too hard, then,' Mr Ringer suggested.

Which was ironical, Mark thought, seeing that ever since that holiday by the sea he had hardly been able to get on with his studies at all. He just could not concentrate on anything.

The Ringers all went to the performance in the Clover Hall on the Monday. The complimentary tickets that Howard Layton handed out were always for the first night because that was the one that was regularly attended by the smallest audience. Things usually improved as you went through the week and Saturday was invariably the best.

Ringer had only two free tickets, so he had to pay for Mark and Angela. They sat in the second row, and Mark was in a highly nervous state as he waited for the curtain to go up. It was an odd sort of experience to bid a fond farewell to a girl in the summer and not see her again until she stepped on to the stage at the village hall in the autumn. He wondered whether such a thing had ever happened before. He discovered that he was sweating under the armpits and his mouth was dry.

When the curtain went up the entire company was revealed, ready to burst into the opening chorus. The only musical accompaniment was provided by Jackie Vernon on one side of the stage going hammer and tongs at the keys of an upright piano. The performers were dressed like pierrots for this first number; it was a song-and-dance routine and the boards creaked under their weight. In fact the front section was no more than a temporary extension which was erected only for such occasions to provide more room for the entertainers. This removable boarding was supported on trestles and tended to sag and whip in a somewhat disconcerting fashion under the feet of the dancers.

Debbie was in the middle of the line and Mark wondered whether she had seen him.

She gave no sign that she had; she just went through the routine with the others. He thought she looked lovely; more so if possible than ever. While she was on stage he was oblivious to all else, watching her every movement, her every expression, as if in a trance.

Later she came on and did a solo act, dressed as a Dutch girl with an apron and clogs. Even the rather sparse audience in the Clover Hall gave her quite an ovation.

'That girl is very good,' Mr Ringer said. 'She really is. And pretty too.'

Even Mrs Ringer had to admit, a trifle grudgingly, that she had a certain way with her. Only Angela remained unimpressed.

'I don't think she's very pretty.'

'Well,' Mr Ringer said, 'I suppose it's all a question of taste. Beauty is in the eye of the beholder. Isn't that what they say?'

If so, Mark thought, it's in my eye when I look at her. I love her. My God, how I love her!

But he said nothing.

While on stage the performers appeared jolly and smiling, living up to the name of Merrymakers, but behind the scenes it was a different story. They grumbled about the meagreness of the audience, about the acoustics of the hall, the rickety stage, the wretched lighting, the untuned piano, everything. Above all they grumbled about the back-stage accommodation.

'It's disgusting,' Jackie Vernon said. 'God knows we're obliged to put up with some pretty foul conditions on tour, but this is the absolute rock bottom.'

'Darling,' Dickie Wilson said, 'I couldn't agree more. But what can one do but grin and bear it?'

What they had to grin and bear were dressing-rooms which were little more than cubicles in a long shed with a corrugated iron roof and sides made of asbestos sheeting. Inside there was a pervading odour of carbide, because the generator for the acetylene lighting stood at one end of it. The only heating was provided by a couple of smoky oil-stoves which added the reek of paraffin to that of the carbide. And there was not even running water, just a few buckets and bowls.

'I don't know why we come here,' Jackie said. 'You'd think the old man could find something better than this to fill in.'

But this was not said in the hearing of Howard Layton. He was as conscious as anyone else of the awfulness of the facilities at the Clover Hall, but where could he have found an alternative to Braddlesham? Looking gloomily at the empty seats on this first night, he wondered whether they would take enough in the week even to cover expenses. He spoke about his misgivings to Gloria, the only person he felt he could confide in.

'Things are getting tight, old girl. If they don't pick up before long I don't know what's going to happen to us.'

But he had no real hope that they would pick up, not with the cinema and broadcasting competing for audiences. Sometimes he wondered whether entertainment of the kind he provided had not had its day. It was a frightening thought; for what else could he do?

'Oh, we'll manage somehow,' Gloria said. 'We'll get by.'

This was the part she always had to play; encouraging him, trying to cheer him up when he was down in the dumps. But in her heart she knew that he was right and the future looked bleak.

To make matters worse there was a near

disaster when one of the trestles gave way as Dickie Wilson was going through his solo routine and precipitated him into the front row of seats. Fortunately, he was not seriously injured, but he was shaken and very indignant.

'It's disgraceful. I could have broken a leg. Somebody ought to be sued for damages. It could have ruined my career.'

What made him all the more resentful was the fact that some yahoos at the back, who were standing on the forms as they usually did to get a better view, started clapping and cheering, as though for them this had been the best part of the performance.

'It's so humiliating,' he said. 'I could cry.' And indeed there were tears in his eyes. It took a good strong tot of whisky to give him the courage to go on again when the treacherous trestle had been replaced and it was possible for the show to continue.

It had been a bad start to the week, and Howard Layton felt that it was no less than an indication that things were going from bad to worse. Again he confided in his wife.

'I have a premonition. This is just the

184

start. There is much worse to come. You'll see.'

She did her best to reassure him. 'You're imagining things, dear. Nothing bad is going to happen.'

But she spoke without conviction; for the truth was that she had that kind of premonition too.

And she was afraid.

16 Plans for Sunday

The days passed and still Mark Ringer had made no contact with Debbie. He wondered whether she was thinking of him and maybe was surprised that he had made no move. Did it seem strange to her that he should not have done so, bearing in mind that there had been a kind of agreement between them at the end of his holiday that they would meet again when The Merrymakers visited Braddlesham?

Perhaps so.

She could of course have contacted him; she knew where he lived. It would have been simple enough for her to walk into the shop and ask for him.

But he knew that she would never do so. She had always insisted that their relationship should remain a secret, and he doubted whether she had changed her mind. And maybe she did not want to see him and was only too glad that he was staying away from her. He remembered the unemotional way she had parted from him; it had certainly not appeared to cause her so much regret as it caused him.

He felt an increasing sense of frustration as the days went by, realizing as he did that at the end of the week the troupe would move on to Sawborough and he would have lost the chance of speaking to her, though he had no idea what he would say when the time came. The more he thought about it the less possible did it seem that there could be any future together for him and Debbie. Briefly they had come together in that unforgettable two weeks by the sea, but now they were again living in two utterly incompatible worlds and there was no common ground between them.

Yet he had to speak to her before the week was out.

And then something happened which

unexpectedly lengthened that period: the Jubilee Hall at Sawborough was destroyed by fire.

Howard Layton felt that he was being dogged by ill-fortune. Sawborough was to have been a two-week run. It was one of their best venues, and he had looked to it to put some money in his pocket. Now he could say goodbye to that. He wondered whether this was the disaster about which he had had the premonition; but he did not think so; he still had the feeling that there was something even worse to come, something truly catastrophic.

He cancelled the accommodation he had booked in Sawborough, since there was no point in moving everything over there now. Tom Simmonds was perfectly willing to let him and the rest of The Merrymakers stay on at the Queen's Head as long as they wished, and Layton just hoped he would have enough money to pay the landlord at the end of the three weeks.

There was no question of putting the show on at the Clover Hall for the extra fortnight; they would have had to pay for the hire and it was unlikely that there would have been more than a handful of customers. One week was enough to drain Braddlesham dry. So the members of the company would have time on their hands to do with as they wished. It was not a prospect any of them seemed to view with pleasure.

'Two more weeks in this dump!' Jackie Vernon said. 'My God!'

The Drings accepted the situation with resignation. They no longer viewed life with any great hopes; if they could just stay in employment, that was about all they asked. They were not getting any younger and they thought of the future with some apprehension. Who wanted a pair of clapped-out specialty dancers?

It was on the Thursday that Debbie put a telephone call through to Longmere Hall from the public kiosk. A man answered, but it was not Hugh Crowther. At a guess she would have said it was the butler.

'Is Mr Crowther at home?' she asked.

'Mr Crowther is in residence, madam.'

'Would you tell him I should like to speak to him?'

'Who shall I say is calling?'

'Tell him it's Debbie.'

'Just Debbie?'

'Yes. He'll know.'

'Very well, madam.'

She had to wait about a minute before Crowther came on the line.

'Is that you, Debbie?'

'Yes, it's me.'

'What do you want?'

'I've got to see you.'

'Look,' he said, 'I don't think that would do any good. I thought you understood; it's all over. We had a good time, but good times don't last for ever.'

'All the same. I have to see you.'

'Why?'

'To talk.'

'There's nothing to talk about.'

'I think there is. And besides, there's something I have to tell you.'

'Tell me now.'

'Not over the phone. It has to be said face to face.'

'Oh, damn it all!'

'How about Sunday? We'll still be here in Braddlesham. We should have been going to Sawborough next week, but the hall was burnt down.'

'Yes, I heard about that.'

'So we're staying on here. Let's say Sunday evening then, shall we? About six o'clock? You needn't come and fetch me. I'll walk.'

'But—'

She did not wait to hear what more he had to say. She hung up on him.

It was the next day when she was waylaid by Mark Ringer. She had been expecting this ever since the arrival of the troupe in Braddlesham, and she could not understand why he had waited so long. She was unaware of the struggle he had been having with himself to summon up the resolution to make the move. It was an act now almost of desperation.

It happened late in the evening when she was leaving the Clover Hall after the performance. All the rest of the company had gone on ahead of her because she had been slow in changing from her stage costume into her normal clothes. Mr and Mrs Layton would have waited for her, but she told them not to bother; she was quite capable of getting to the Queen's Head on her own; she was not afraid of bogeymen even in the dark.

But it was no bogeyman who was waiting for her in the lane outside the hall. There were no street-lamps in Braddlesham, but it was not completely dark because of the moon, which was giving some light; and she could see the shadowy figure which suddenly appeared in front of her, barring the way. She had guessed who it was even before he spoke; then she was sure.

'Debbie!'

His voice sounded hoarse, perhaps because he had been standing around in the damp night air, but she recognized it easily enough. She had been forced to come to a stop, but he had not touched her; he was just standing there, not moving.

'So it's you, Mark,' she said. 'At last. Why did it take you so long?'

He knew what she meant. 'I had to see you alone. I've been waiting for the chance, but you've always been with other people.'

'Well, that's the way it is.'

'I was at the first night.'

'Yes, I saw you. Did you like the show?'

'I thought you were marvellous.'

She gave a laugh. 'So you're still crazy about me?'

'You're never out of my mind.'

'Now you're exaggerating. You shouldn't make too much of what happened last summer, you know.'

191

He was chilled by her words. 'Didn't it mean anything to you?'

'Of course it meant something. But let's not build this up into one of the great romances of all time. All right, I liked being with you; I enjoyed everything we did together, everything. But it's not the be-all and end-all, is it? Life has to go on. We have to think of other things.'

'Are you saying you don't love me?'

'Oh,' she said, 'why do you have to make everything so difficult? Why can't you just take things and leave things?'

'Perhaps because I'm not made like that.'

Suddenly she flung her arms round his neck and kissed him. He held her close, and it was the way he remembered it from the summer; the way he wanted it to be. But the embrace was brief. She pulled away from him and he had to let her go.

'So maybe I do love you, Mark,' she said. 'Maybe I do at that. What is love after all? But it's no use, is it? I mean what can we do about it? You've got nothing and I've got nothing. Except hopes. And you can't live on them. We have to look at the situation like sensible adults, not like a pair of moonstruck adolescents.'

Again her words struck a chill to his heart. He could not understand how she could treat so coolly something which to him was an obsession, obliterating all else. He was lost for words.

'Now,' she said briskly, as though putting all that nonsense behind her, 'I really must go. They'll be wondering what's happened to me and maybe sending out a search-party, thinking I've been murdered or something.'

'You shouldn't joke about things like that.'

'Oh, it'll never happen to me. I'm not the type.'

'We've got to meet again,' he said. 'There's so little time left. You'll be leaving on Sunday.'

'No; that's off. Now that the hall at Sawborough has been burnt down there's no point in going there, so we're staying on at the Queen's Head for another couple of weeks. We'll have time on our hands. They're all moaning about it.'

He could hardly believe fate had been so kind. If she was free from the tyranny of the stage it would be almost like it had been at the seaside. They could meet somewhere far enough away from

Braddlesham to be confident of not being seen together by anyone who knew them. But it had to be arranged.

'Look, Debbie,' he said. 'I've got to talk to you somewhere private. It'll have to be Sunday.' It would be the first day of her freedom. 'I know a place. I used to play there with some boys when I was younger. It's an old black barn which is hardly used now. It's just off the Heyworth Road, about a quarter of a mile from the village. We could meet there Sunday evening. What do you say?'

She thought about it. She knew the building he meant; she had travelled past it on several occasions and she would pass it when she walked out to Longmere Hall for the interview with Hugh Crowther. So things would fit in quite conveniently.

'Well?' he said.

'All right. But I shan't be able to get there before seven, and maybe later, because there's something else I have to do first.'

She did not tell him what the something was; she knew too well it would have upset him if he had known.

'Fine,' Mark said. He was elated by the fact that she should so readily have agreed to the plan. He had expected her to take a deal of persuading; but she had seemed to indicate that she really wanted to have this meeting with him. So perhaps her feeling for him was stronger than she cared to admit. 'I'll be there at seven and I'll wait until you come.'

'Very well,' she said. 'But don't go building any castles in the air, because there's still no way this can come to anything.'

She reached up again and gave him another kiss, and then she was gone. He could hear the clicking of her heels on the tarmac as she merged into the gloom and vanished from his sight.

In spite of her parting words he went home in high spirits. They would work something out. He was quite sure of it.

17 Two Persons

Detective Inspector Drake of the County CID had no very wide experience of murder investigations. Murders were rare in his area of operations, and the last one had been two years ago when a gamekeeper named Horrocks was shot by a poacher named Sims. That had been a pretty simple case, and Sims had duly been hanged for his crime. It was all very well to shoot somebody else's pheasants, but when it came to shooting the keeper of those birds, that was carrying things a little too far.

Walter Drake was forty-two years old and had a sprinkling of grey in his hair. His wife told him that it made him look rather distinguished; it was a mark of maturity. Drake had doubts about the distinguished look but the maturity was undeniable; it was something we all came to if we lived long enough and there was no credit in it. He was a big man, heavy-featured and not much given to laughter. The murder of Deborah Layton saddened him; a pretty young girl like that should have had many happy years of life ahead of her.

The body had been found on the Monday morning, but the police surgeon estimated that death had occurred the previous evening. Mr and Mrs Layton said their daughter had gone out late in the afternoon on the Sunday. She had not arrived back at the Queen's Head, the inn where they were staying, when the Laytons retired to bed. This was rather early and they were not at all worried about her because she was an independent sort of girl and it would not have been the first time she had stayed out late without letting them know where she was. However, when she had not returned in the morning they became uneasy and Mr Layton went to the Braddlesham Police-Station and reported the matter to Sergeant Radford, who was in charge there.

There had been no need to make a search for the missing girl, however, for while Layton was still at the station a farm labourer named Leverett arrived on a bicycle in a state of great excitement with the news that he had found the body of a young female lying on a pile of hay in an old barn on his employer's land. It became Howard Layton's distressing duty to identify the body as that of his dearly loved daughter.

The cause of death was all too apparent; the knife was still in the body, only the handle protruding. But the handle was no ordinary one; it was of gold, set with jewels; without doubt a collector's item. Detective Inspector Drake, appearing later on the scene, felt that it ought not to be too difficult to find the owner of a knife as unusual as this one. And perhaps when the owner of the murder weapon was found one would find the murderer also. Though it was strange that he should have left it with the victim.

When the body had been taken away to the mortuary he began the business of interviewing and questioning, assisted by Detective Sergeant Barling, an ambitious young police officer who was rather pleased to be involved in a murder case. It made a welcome change from the usual run of lesser crimes.

At the Queen's Head a tearful Mrs Layton was being comforted by Mrs Dring, a member of The Merrymakers concert party, so Drake was told.

'Are all the members of the company staying here?' he asked.

Layton told him they were.

'I shall want to question all of them, of course. But first I'd like to take a look at your daughter's room.'

Layton conducted him to the room. Drake felt sorry for the man; he looked haggard, as though all the cares of the world had fallen on his shoulders. The sight of the room which his daughter had occupied appeared to affect him deeply; he sat down on the bed and held his head in his long bony fingers.

'I'm sorry about this, sir,' Drake said, 'but it has to be done. We have to look through your daughter's things.'

Layton raised his head and looked at the inspector. 'I understand. Do what you have to do.'

Drake gave a nod to Barling, who started sorting through the worldly possessions that the dead girl had left behind. They did not amount to a great deal, though some of the clothes were fairly new and of good quality.

Drake spoke to Layton. 'Did she have a boyfriend? A lover perhaps?'

Layton gave an emphatic shake of the head. 'Oh, no, nothing of that sort. She was completely absorbed by her work. She was so talented. Singing, dancing, acting; she could do it all. Her mother and I had great hopes for her future. We were both confident that she had a very successful career ahead of her. All gone now, all gone.' His voice was shaking with emotion. 'Such a sweet girl. Only eighteen, you know, and no vice in her. A jewel, a priceless jewel.'

'I'm sorry,' Drake said again; and he meant it. He pitied Layton. He had a daughter of his own, just turned sixteen. He could imagine how he would have felt if she had been murdered.

Barling's voice broke in upon his reflections, harsh as a crow. 'What's this?' He was holding a thin gold chain with a small figurine in the shape of a black cat attached to it.

Layton glanced at it. 'Something she picked up during the summer season. It's a good luck charm.'

'Didn't bring her much luck, did it?' Barling said.

Drake frowned at him. It was the kind of unfeeling remark one might have expected from him; good at his job but lacking in humanity. Yet if he had told Barling so, he was certain the man would not have understood what he was talking about. Some people were like that; as insensitive as stones.

'What time was it when she went out yesterday?' Drake asked.

'I don't know precisely, but it must have

been rather late because we were talking to her at four o'clock. Then she said she was going to her room.'

'Did she say where she was going?'

'No. And we didn't see her leave.'

'Didn't she mention at all that she was going out?'

'No. The fact is we didn't know she'd gone until my wife came up to speak to her about something and found she wasn't here.'

'Were you surprised she should go out without telling you?'

'Not really. She was like that.'

'Thoughtless?'

'Well, no; I wouldn't say that. Not wilfully so.' Layton obviously did not wish to imply any criticism of the dead girl. 'Happy-go-lucky, you know. Always doing things on the spur of the moment, just as the whim took her.'

Drake heard an exclamation from Barling. 'Aha!'

He glanced at the sergeant, who was sorting through a suitcase that had been resting on top of the wardrobe. Now he was holding in his right hand a photograph which had apparently been in it.

'Mr Layton,' Barling said, 'I thought

you told us your daughter didn't have a boyfriend.'

'That's so.'

Barling turned the photograph so that Layton could see it. There were two people in the picture, a young man and a girl. The girl had turned her head as though to say something to her companion. There was a kind of intimacy in the act, which the camera had caught.

'Isn't this a photo of her?'

Layton stared at the photograph in obvious astonishment. 'Why, yes, it is.'

'So who is that with her?'

'I don't know.'

'You're quite sure you don't?'

'Of course I'm sure. To my certain knowledge I've never seen that person.'

'She never told you about him?'

'No. Perhaps it's just somebody who happened to be walking beside her when the picture was taken.'

'Why would she keep a picture of herself and a perfect stranger?'

Layton said nothing. Drake could see that he was not only surprised; he was shocked. There could be no doubt that this had come as a revelation to him; and an unwelcome one.

'It seems to me that your daughter didn't tell you everything,' Barling said. 'We'll have to see if we can find out who this young fellow is. He might be able to help us.' He glanced at Drake for confirmation. 'Wouldn't you say so, Inspector?'

Drake replied curtly: 'Of course, of course.' What Barling said was true, but did he have to speak in that way, almost as if gloating? It was like hitting a man when he was down.

He took the photograph from the sergeant and examined it closely. There was nothing to show where or when it had been taken. There was no photographer's name on the back. He consulted Layton.

'Have you any idea where this was taken?'

Layton answered in a subdued voice, quite unlike his normal stagey boom. All the spirit seemed to have gone out of him as he sat hunched on the bed. 'It must have been last summer when we were doing a season at the Pier Pavilion in Sandport. Debbie sprained her ankle and was out of action for a few weeks. She had a lot of time on her hands and we didn't see so much of her.'

Drake handed the photograph back to Barling. 'That's a job for you, George. First thing tomorrow. Drive down there and see if you can find the photographer and get some information out of him.'

He had a private talk with Dickie Wilson next, and from this elegant young man he got a different picture of Miss Deborah Layton than he had from her father.

'She was a little bitch, you know.'

'I didn't know,' Drake said. 'Tell me.'

Wilson told him. It was apparent that he had no inhibitions about speaking ill of the dead.

'She was not all she appeared to be. Oh, she looked innocent enough, as if butter wouldn't melt in her mouth, but you can't always go by looks, can you?'

'That's true,' Drake said.

'Most people were taken in, of course.'

'But not you?'

'Not on your life. She tried her wiles on me, but I wasn't having any. Just think what complications that might have caused. So I just told her where to get off in no uncertain terms. She didn't like it. It was a blow to her ego, you see. Thought she could twist any man round her little finger. Found it didn't work with yours truly.'

'Attracted to men, was she?'

'My word, yes. Not everybody could see it, but I could. I could read her like a book. I could see just what she was; a fake; on the outside all sweetness and light, but inside black as the pit. An angel to look at but a devil under the skin.'

Drake thought Wilson was laying it on a bit thick. He wondered whether in fact it had been Dickie who had made a pass at the girl and had been rebuffed. It might have been his ego that had been pricked; which would have been a reason for his spitefulness. He doubted whether Miss Layton had been such a thoroughly bad lot as Wilson would have had him believe or such a paragon as her father had imagined. She had probably been a mixture of good and bad; most people were.

'I understand she had a lot of talent.'

Wilson gave a smirk. 'To hear some people talk you'd think she was a bloody marvel. She wasn't, though. Oh, she wasn't bad, I'll grant you. She could sing a bit and dance a bit, but the only reason she got the top billing in this company was because she had the manager for a father. None of us others could compete with that.'

Drake saw that here was another reason for Dickie Wilson's spite: professional jealousy. Could it have been a motive for murder? A possibility, but hardly likely. And if Wilson had killed Miss Layton he would surely not have revealed his dislike for her quite so candidly.

Still, it was something to bear in mind.

When he talked to the Drings he found a pair of very worried people. It was not so much, he gathered, the mere fact of the murder, though they were terribly upset about that and so sorry for Howard and Gloria, but the possible consequences of it. They feared the break-up of The Merrymakers and the loss of their employment. There had been ominous signs that all was not well even before this unfortunate happening, and it might prove the last straw.

As to the murder, they could not think why anyone should wish to kill such a nice young girl. You would not have thought she had an enemy in the world.

'You liked her, did you?'

'Oh, yes,' Mrs Dring said. 'She was

always so jolly and pleasant, wasn't she, Des?'

'A real tonic,' Dring said. 'Did you good just to look at her.'

'What sort of performer was she?'

'The best,' Mrs Dring said. 'Wasted in the kind of show we put on, and the audiences we play to; that's the truth of it. Should have been much higher up in the theatre world. Might have been, too, if she'd lived.'

'She wasn't half as good as she thought she was,' Jackie Vernon said. 'But of course that would have taken some doing.'

Drake had found Miss Vernon and Miss Maxted in the room they shared. He had asked them to wait there until he could have a talk with them. He thought Miss Vernon seemed very sure of herself; the sort of person who would face the world with confidence. There was a kind of toughness about her that he did not find particularly endearing.

The other woman, the fluffy blonde, looked nervous, a bit intimidated. Drake was not surprised; some people always reacted like that when questioned by a police officer; it did not necessarily mean they had a guilty conscience. Hardened criminals on the other hand, aware of having committed any number of offences, could be completely brazen under interrogation.

'Thought a lot of herself, did she?'

Miss Vernon gave a toss of the head; a very sleek black-haired head, Drake noted, trimmed like a man's.

'That would be putting it mildly. Conceited little minx. And mischievous with it. Amused her to cause trouble in the troupe. That's so, isn't it, Maudie?'

Miss Maxted looked uncomfortable. 'Well, I suppose she liked a bit of fun.'

'Fun's all right. But when it gets to be more than that it can become plain vicious.'

'Are you saying Miss Layton was a vicious person?'

Jackie Vernon appeared to sense that she might have gone a bit too far and that a slight retraction might be advisable. 'No, I wouldn't say that exactly. I'm just saying she would do things without consideration for other people's feelings. Just for the hell of it.'

'Ah!' Drake said.

He wondered whether there were not

two persons named Deborah Layton lying dead in the mortuary; two persons who looked exactly alike but had totally different characters.

18 Odd Customer

'I have had a visit from a policeman,' Mr Ringer announced as the family sat down to their midday meal on the Tuesday. 'He came into the shop this morning.'

'What did he want?' Mrs Ringer asked.

'Oh, it seems they're making inquiries all round the village, trying to find whether anyone saw that poor girl on Sunday afternoon or evening. I suppose they want to know how she came to be in that old barn. It's not the sort of place you expect her to go to. I'm afraid I wasn't able to help. Fact is, I haven't seen her since we went to the opening performance at the Clover Hall.'

'I can hardly believe it,' Mrs Ringer said. 'She was so full of life then, and now she's dead. I feel for her parents.'

Mr Ringer helped himself to pickles

from a jar to go with his cold beef. 'Yes, they must really be distressed. They thought the world of her, you know. Mr Layton told me. They felt sure she would have a great career on the stage; become a star.'

Angela sniffed. 'She never would have. They were just fooling themselves.' She should have been at school but had complained of an attack of migraine at breakfast and had been allowed to stay at home.

Mark snapped at her sharply: 'How do you know she wouldn't?'

'Anyone could see. She wasn't all that good.'

'I don't think you're being quite fair,' Mr Ringer said. 'Everybody I've spoken to about her thought she was very talented.'

'Yes, but what do they know about that sort of thing?'

'As much as you do,' Mark said. 'I'd like to see you have a shot at it. Get you up on the stage and you'd be lost.'

'Well, it's not my living, is it?'

'Lucky for you.'

'Anyway,' Mr Ringer said, 'it doesn't make any difference now how good she was or was not. It's all over for her.

It's such a shame something like that should happen to someone so young and promising.'

'She probably asked for it,' Angela said.

'Now whatever makes you say that, dear?' Mrs Ringer asked.

'I'd say she was a bad lot; the sort that would be likely to get herself into trouble.'

At this Mark suddenly flared up. 'Shut your mouth, you stupid little bitch. You know nothing about her.'

There was a moment or two of shocked silence after this outburst. Then Mrs Ringer said:

'Really, Mark! That's hardly the way to speak to your sister.'

'So why does she say such rotten things about someone who can't defend herself? It's mean and spiteful and I won't listen to it.'

'My, my!' Angela said. 'Aren't we touchy! Anybody might think you were in love with her.'

Mark pushed his chair back from the table and stood up. 'I can't take any more of this. I'm going.' He walked to the door and pulled it open.

'But Mark!' Mrs Ringer protested. 'You

haven't eaten anything.'

'I've lost my appetite.'

He went out of the room and slammed the door behind him.

Mr Ringer was shaking his head in bewilderment. 'I don't know what's come over that boy these last few days. He's been like a bear with a sore head. Not like himself at all.'

'I just hope he isn't sickening for something,' Mrs Ringer said.

Angela gave another sniff. 'He's just being beastly, that's all.'

Mrs Ringer turned on her. 'And you shouldn't say things to annoy him. It seems to me sometimes that you do it on purpose, just to stir up a row.'

'Oh, so it's my fault now, is it? So I'm not to be allowed to speak my mind. Well, that's nice, isn't it? Why do you always take his side against me?'

'You know I don't do that.'

'You do, you do. And it's horrid.' She pushed her plate away from her in a pettish gesture and began to cry.

Mr Ringer stared at the beef and pickles on his own plate and wished he had never mentioned the policeman.

Detective Sergeant George Barling arrived back from the seaside early in the afternoon with nothing helpful to report. He had had no great difficulty in tracing the photographer he was looking for; a man named Sidney Pinching who had a small shop and studio in one of the minor streets of the town. When Barling showed him the photograph he recognized the situation where it had been taken; it was his regular pitch during the summer season.

'Do a lot of business there. All on spec, of course. Still, there's plenty of people as want to see what they look like walking along the prom. It's human nature, I suppose.'

Pinching was a little wisp of a man with jet-black hair and a Vandyke beard which he probably thought gave him an artistic appearance. He was most obliging and seemed genuinely regretful that he could not be of more assistance to the sergeant.

'Don't keep records of all the customers, see? Don't even get their names and addresses unless they order by post after they get home. Most just walk into the shop, show the card I give them when I take the snap and ask for the photo.

This would be likely one of that sort. Haven't a clue who the young couple are. Sorry.'

'So that's all you can tell me?'

'Afraid so. What's it all about anyway?'

'Just a routine inquiry,' Barling said. 'Thanks for the help.'

'What help?' Pinching asked.

Drake gave a shrug when Barling reported back to him at Braddlesham. He took the photograph from the sergeant and put it in his pocket.

'That's the way it goes. You win some; you lose some.'

'Nothing new turned up?'

'No. We've been asking round. Nobody's been any help. None of them seem to have seen the girl after she left the Queen's Head on Sunday.'

'Somebody saw her,' Barling said.

'The one who stuck the knife in her, you mean? Well, he's not likely to come forward of his own accord. We've just got to winkle him out. What we need is a break.'

The break came later in the afternoon. A young woman walked into Braddlesham

Police-Station and said she had some information to give. She said her name was Emily Grimes and she was a housemaid at Longmere Hall.

'It's been worrying me,' she said. 'In the end I felt it was my public duty to come to you.'

She was quite tall and slim, and she might have been rather attractive if it had not been for her nose, which was long and pointed. While not being in the outrageous class of Cyrano de Bergerac's, it was greatly out of proportion and spoiled the overall effect. It was probably distressing for her every time she looked in a mirror.

Inspector Drake and Sergeant Barling were both at the police station at the time and were in fact being refreshed with tea and buns supplied by Sergeant Radford's wife. Radford himself was with them, and a less self-assured woman than Emily Grimes might have been overawed by this intimidating trio of large officers of the law, one in uniform and two in plain clothes.

Drake introduced himself and Sergeant Barling. 'No doubt you already know Sergeant Radford?'

'By sight,' she replied primly. 'I have

never had any dealings with the police. Until now.'

Drake invited her to sit down; which she did; very upright on a plain wooden chair.

'You say something has been worrying you. What would that be?'

'The murder. I read about it in the paper, see? And I heard as how you was asking round the village for anybody what saw the girl on the Sunday after she left the Queen's Head.'

She paused, rubbed her nose, looked at the inspector.

'Yes?' Drake prompted.

'I saw her.'

'You did?'

'Yes; she came up to Longmere that evening. It'd be about six o'clock. I let her in because Saunders, the butler, wasn't there, being as he'd got the day off. She said Mr Crowther was expecting her, so I took her to the library where he was.'

'Mr Crowther being your employer?'

'Yes, sir.'

'Man of about thirty or so,' Radford explained. 'Bachelor. Well-to-do. Comes and goes.'

Drake acknowledged this information with a nod and turned again to Miss Grimes. 'How long did she stay?'

'Not all that long. Might have been about three quarters of an hour.'

'I suppose you don't know why she came to see Mr Crowther?'

'No, not really. But it wasn't the first time she'd been there. He brought her in his car about a year ago, and they had tea in the drawing-room. And I did hear as how he took her up to his place in London last summer.'

'So Mr Crowther was well acquainted with Miss Layton?'

'Oh, yes, sir.'

'Now tell me,' Drake said, 'have you any idea what Mr Crowther and Miss Layton talked about in the library?'

'No, sir, of course not.' Miss Grimes gave the impression of being somewhat offended by the suggestion. 'I've never been an eavesdropper. And besides, you couldn't hear what anybody was saying on the other side of one of them oak doors even if you had your ear pressed right up against it.'

Drake wondered whether Miss Grimes was speaking from experience. How would she have known otherwise?

'Howsomever,' she said, 'I did happen to be passing when it sounded like they was having a real old set-to. Shouting like. Though even then I couldn't make out what was said.'

'But you think they might have been quarrelling?'

'That's what it sounded like.'

'Did you see Miss Layton leave?'

'No; but I heard the front door bang, so I reckon she must've let herself out. And then, not long after, Mr Crowther went off in his car.'

'Ah!' Drake said.

'There's something else,' Miss Grimes said.

'Yes?'

'There's a paper-knife missing from the library.'

'A paper-knife?'

'Well, not a proper one, but that's what Mr Crowther used it for.'

'Can you describe it?'

'Yes, sir. It's got a pointed blade about ten inches long and a gold handle with a lot of jewels in it.'

Drake caught a meaningful glance from Barling. There could be no doubt that Miss

Grimes was describing the murder weapon. And there had been no description of it in the press. She was obviously telling the truth.

'When did you discover that it was gone?'

'Soon after Mr Crowther left. I went into the library to see if there was anything needed doing and I noticed it at once because it always used to be lying on the table he used as a desk. It wasn't there no more.'

'Do you think Mr Crowther took it with him?'

But she refused to give an opinion on that. 'I don't know, sir.'

'Tell me,' Drake said, 'why did you wait until now before coming to tell us all this?'

'I didn't think it was my place, sir, being only a servant. I was waiting for him to come and tell you hisself.'

'You mean Mr Crowther?'

'Yes, sir. But when it didn't look like he was going to do anything I thought maybe I ought to take the matter into my own hands.'

'Did you mention this to Mr Crowther?'

'No, sir.'

'Why not?'

'I didn't like to.'

'How about the other servants? I suppose there are others at the hall.'

'Oh, yes, sir. But like I said, Mr Saunders was away and none of the others saw Miss Layton come or leave; they was all at the back.'

'And you didn't tell them?'

'No, sir. I didn't see as how it was any of their business.'

Drake thought Miss Grimes was an odd customer. He wondered whether she had given the true reason why she had decided to come to the police and tell what she knew or whether there was another motive. But either way, she had given them a lead and possibly a suspect; and the inspector was not the man to look a gift horse in the mouth.

'Is Mr Crowther at home now?'

'He was when I left.'

'Then I think,' Drake said, 'it's time we had a little chat with him.'

He thought he saw a gleam come into Miss Grimes's eye, but he could not be certain, and her face was innocent of any expression. Certainly an odd sort of customer; no doubt about that.

19 Idle Rich

Drake took Barling with him when he paid his call on Hugh Crowther at Longmere Hall. He had offered to give Miss Grimes a lift back, but she had refused; she said she had ridden down to the village on her bicycle and she could quite well ride back on it. Besides, she had some shopping to do.

It was the butler, Saunders, a large stout man with a majestic bearing, who opened the door to them. He kept them waiting in the entrance hall while he went away to see whether his employer could spare them a little of his time. He returned very shortly to conduct them to the library where Mr Crowther would be pleased to see them.

Drake had his doubts about the pleasure, but Crowther gave no indication of being at all displeased by the arrival of the two detectives. He welcomed them cordially enough and invited them to sit down.

The library was a large oak-panelled room with shelves of books and an Adam fireplace in which a log fire was burning. The chairs in which Drake and Barling seated themselves were upholstered in soft leather.

'I think, sir,' Drake said, 'you may have already guessed why we are here.'

'Tell me all the same,' Crowther said. 'I may have guessed wrong.'

He seemed faintly amused, which annoyed Drake. This was a smoothie, the inspector decided, and he disliked smoothies, especially rich ones. He noted the elegance of Crowther's attire, casual but undoubtedly expensive, and the plentiful dark hair which contrasted sharply with Drake's own thinning crop.

'We are here,' he said, 'because one of your servants tells us that a murdered girl, Miss Deborah Layton, was here last Sunday evening.'

Crowther smiled slightly. 'The servant you are referring to wouldn't by any chance be Emily Grimes, would it?'

'That is her name.'

'It may interest you to learn that she is under notice to leave. For insolence.'

It did interest Drake. It explained why Miss Grimes had felt it her duty to come to the police. Spite was as good a motive as any. But it made no difference.

'Are you telling me she was lying about Miss Layton?'

'Oh, no; that was the truth.'

'Then why,' Drake asked, 'didn't you come to us yourself? You must have known we were making inquiries.'

Crowther answered coolly: 'I saw no point in rushing things. I felt sure you would come to me eventually. It amounts to the same thing in the end.'

Out of the corner of his eye Drake observed a movement by Barling suggesting he might have been inclined to attack Crowther. He himself was infuriated by the man's attitude, but he knew that nothing would be gained by losing one's temper. He wondered whether it might be possible to charge Crowther with obstructing the police or withholding information. But he doubted whether either charge would stick, especially if he was willing to co-operate now.

'So Miss Layton was here?'

'Yes.'

'At what time?'

'A little after six o'clock.'

'Would you care to tell me what she came for?'

Crowther's answer surprised him. 'To have a row with me.'

'She came to have a row with you?'

'Well, not perhaps with that express purpose. But I fancy she guessed that was what it might lead to.'

Drake said carefully: 'I think, sir, it might help if you were to tell us what precisely your relationship with Miss Layton was.'

Crowther leaned back in his chair, crossed his legs, extracted a cigarette from a gold case and lighted it, taking his time.

'I suppose you might say we were lovers. For a while.'

'She was very young,' Drake said, trying to keep the note of disapproval out of his voice and not altogether succeeding.

'She was old enough for that.'

Barling put a word in. 'When was it?'

Crowther turned his head languidly to look at the sergeant. 'When was what?'

'When you were lovers.'

'Last August. She spent a couple of weeks in my London house. We went around together, took in some shows, that sort of thing.'

'And that was the end of it?'

'Yes. Until last Sunday I hadn't seen her since.'

'You told us she came to have a row,' Drake said. 'What would that have been about?'

'She had ambitions for a career on the stage. I have some connections in the London theatre world and I offered to help; introduce her to people, get auditions for her, and so on. But nothing came of it and she blamed me. She accused me of making promises I couldn't keep just to get her on the hook. I said that wasn't true; I really had done my best for her but nobody could guarantee to make her a star and maybe she just hadn't got it in her. Of course she didn't like that at all and it gradually built up into something of a slanging match.'

Which no doubt was what Emily Grimes had heard, Drake reflected; the two of them shouting at each other.

'And then,' Crowther said, 'she suddenly switched her attack. She said she was going to have a baby and what did I propose doing about it?'

Drake looked at him in surprise. 'She said that?'

'Yes, I got the impression that she

225

thought I ought to marry her, and she wasn't terribly pleased when I suggested she should find a good abortionist. It seemed to drive her really mad, and she snatched up a knife I used to keep on that table for slitting open envelopes and made a lunge at me with it. She really meant it, too; she was screaming curses at me and it was all I could do avoid the blade. This went on for a minute or two until I managed to grab her wrist and stop her thrusting at me with the knife. That seemed to take the heart out of her, and she stopped struggling and began to cry. I let go of her wrist and she went out of the room like a shot, taking the knife with her. I heard the front door slam and I knew she'd left the house.'

'You're telling us she took the knife with her?' Drake said, disbelievingly.

'Yes.'

'Why would she do that?'

'I don't know. Maybe she thought she'd take it as a kind of compensation for what she figured was my failure to get her what she wanted. It's pretty valuable. Or she may just have been in such a state that she didn't realize she was still holding it. I don't know. All I know is she took it.'

'Then what did you do?'

'I had an appointment to keep, so after she'd gone I got the car out and drove away.'

'Where was this appointment?'

'It was with a friend of mine, Brewster Cawthorne of Dalby Manor, about ten miles from here. We'd arranged to play billiards on his table. You can check on that if you like.'

'We will,' Drake said.

Sergeant Barling came in again, harsh-voiced, suspicious. 'You're sure you didn't go after Miss Layton, catch her up, drag her into the barn and stab her to death with the knife? You could have done that and then gone on to play billiards with your friend.'

'Is that what you think?'

'I'm asking you—sir.'

'Well, I didn't. Why would I want to kill her?'

'You'd had a quarrel. She tried to stab you, so you say. And she was pregnant by you.'

Crowther gave a contemptuous laugh. 'There's no proof of that. If she was going to have a child anyone might have been the father. She was a tart. There was a boy she was going round with in Sandport; he could have given her the kid.'

Drake said: 'You saw this boy?'

'Oh, yes, I saw him. She was with him at the races and they joined my party.'

Drake pulled the photograph out of his pocket and showed it to Crowther. 'Is that the boy?'

'Yes, that's him.'

'And you know who he is?'

'Of course I do. I've played cricket against him. He's a Braddlesham boy. Young Mark Ringer; son of the grocer.'

Drake felt like kicking himself. It had never occurred to him that the boy in the photograph lived in this village. If he had just shown the picture to Sergeant Radford he would probably have identified him at once and there would have been no need to send George Barling on that unproductive trip to the seaside.

He cast a rather sheepish glance at Barling, who stared back at him, stony-faced. 'It looks as if we have another call to make.'

'Yes,' Barling said, 'it does, doesn't it?'

They got up from their chairs.

Crowther raised an eyebrow. 'You're leaving?'

'Yes,' Drake said. 'Thank you for your co-operation, sir. Much appreciated.'

'So you're not going to arrest me?' Crowther asked, mockingly.

'No, sir. Not at this juncture.'

'I'd like to put the cuffs on that bastard,' Barling said when they were on their way. 'Arrogant swine.'

'You just don't like the idle rich,' Drake told him.

'True. In my book everybody should work for a living. And I still think he could've done it.'

'You mean he may have taken the knife from her and stabbed her with it?'

'We've only his word that she ever had it.'

'But think about it, George. What sane man would leave his own easily identifiable knife sticking in the victim? He'd have taken it away.'

'People do some odd things. Pity there weren't any prints on the handle. Somebody must've wiped it.'

'Well,' Drake said, 'maybe we'll know more when we've had a talk with young Mr Ringer.'

20 Long Day

It was six o'clock when they arrived at the grocer's shop, and Alfred Ringer was just shutting up for the night, the last customer having been served. He looked surprised when Inspector Drake introduced himself and Sergeant Barling.

'But there's been a constable here. It is about that poor girl who was murdererd, I suppose?'

'Yes, it is about her, Mr Ringer; but it's your son we'd like to speak to this time. Is he at home?'

'Mark? Why, yes, he's in. But what can he tell you?' A note of concern had crept into Ringer's voice and he peered anxiously at the inspector through his gold-rimmed glasses.

'That's what we'd like to know,' Drake said.

'I suppose you'd better come in, then. I'll just bolt this door.'

He did so and then led the way to the residential part of the establishment. Mrs

Ringer was setting the table in the dining-room, but she stopped abruptly, some knives and forks in her hand, when the three men appeared in the passageway.

'My dear,' Ringer said, 'these people are police detectives. They've come to talk to Mark. Is he in his work-room?'

'I think so, but—'

'Would you go and fetch him? I'll take these gentlemen into the front room. I think it would be best. This way, please.'

He had to light a lamp. A fire was laid with paper, kindling and coal; but it had not been lit and the room was chilly, smelling of furniture-polish. There were two windows looking out on to the street, and he drew the thick velvet curtains to ensure privacy. He had just finished doing this when Mrs Ringer came in with Mark, who looked pale and nervous.

After brief preliminaries Drake came quickly to the point. He took the photograph from his pocket and showed it to the boy.

'I believe this is a photo of you.'

Mark glanced at it and answered in a faint voice: 'Yes.'

'And the girl is Miss Deborah Layton?'

'Yes.'

'The picture, of course, was taken last summer at Sandport?'

Again, faintly: 'Yes.'

'Oh, Mark!' It was Mrs Ringer; shocked, distressed.

Drake, ignoring the interjection, still addressed himself to the boy. 'Is there anything you'd like to tell us now?'

This time the answer was uttered so softly it was scarcely audible; but it was still the one word: 'Yes.'

'Good,' Drake said. 'Now take your time. You'd better sit down.'

Mark seemed to grope his way to an armchair, feeling for it with his hand like a blind man. He sat down suddenly as though his legs had given way.

'I'm glad you've come,' he said. 'I've been expecting you. It's been driving me out of my mind; the suspense, the waiting. So in a way it's a relief, you see.'

He paused, put a hand to his mouth, the hand shaking.

'Go on,' Drake said, softly.

'I killed her, of course. That's what you wanted to know, isn't it?'

Mrs Ringer gave a cry, as though of pain. 'Mark!'

Alfred Ringer was just staring at his son

in disbelief, saying nothing.

'I didn't mean to, though,' Mark said. 'It was an accident.'

'An accident?' Drake said.

'Yes. You've got to believe me. I would never have harmed her purposely. I loved her.'

Drake gave a nod. 'I think you'd better tell us the whole story. How did you come to be in the barn?'

'We'd arranged that. Last Friday, it was. I waited for Debbie after the performance at the Clover Hall and spoke to her alone. That was when I suggested we should meet again on the Sunday to talk things over.'

'What things?'

'The future of our relationship, what to do, how to work things out. I'd tried to think of somewhere private and the old barn seemed a suitable place. She said she couldn't get there before seven because there was something she had to do first.'

'Did she say what it was?'

'No. I said I'd go there and wait until she came. Which is what I did. I took a torch and got there a bit before seven and waited in the dark. In fact I didn't have to wait long; not more than about ten minutes. Then I heard her voice. She was calling my name. I switched the torch on and went to the door to show her the way in. When she was inside I put the torch on the floor. It gave enough light where we were standing, though most of the place was in shadow.

'Well, then we began talking about things, and I thought she seemed a bit strange.'

'In what way?'

'Excited, perhaps; though it was more than that. When we were talking it was as if half her mind was on something else. If I asked her a question she'd answer at random or maybe not at all. Then suddenly she said: "I'm going to have a baby. What am I to do?" '

Mrs Ringer gave a gasp. She and her husband were staring fixedly at their son. They seemed to be stupefied by what he was saying.

'I was stunned,' Mark said. 'It was a complication I'd never dreamed about.'

'Did she say you were the father?'

'She didn't have to, did she?'

No, Drake thought, she didn't have to; not to him. He was not the same as Hugh Crowther. He was young, gullible,

234

altruistic. It was probable that the girl had led him on.

'I couldn't think straight,' Mark said. 'I was so bowled over. It made everything so different. And what could I do? I hadn't even got any money.'

Sergeant Barling broke in with his harsh, sardonic voice: 'So she was a nuisance to you? Someone you wanted out of the way?'

Mark stared at him. 'No; it wasn't like that at all. Didn't I tell you I loved her? She was the whole world to me. Everything.'

'Yet you killed her.'

'Yes, I killed her.' He seemed to choke on the words. They were like a sob in the throat.

'Tell us about the knife,' Drake said.

'The knife! Oh, yes. She was wearing a belted raincoat with deep pockets, and suddenly she pulled the knife out of one of them and held it with the point towards her. "I'm going to kill myself," she said. "It'll be the best for both of us. There's no future for me, none at all. I'll make an end of it now." She put her other hand on the knife-handle then, so that she was gripping it with both hands, and I really believed

235

she was going to do what she said. I was horrified. I knew I had to stop her. I made a grab at the knife and she stepped back to avoid me. There was a pile of hay on the floor behind her, and she tripped on it and fell over backwards. I was following closely, and I tripped too and fell on top of her. I didn't even touch the knife with my hands, but she was still holding it with the point towards her, and my chest hit it and drove it into her. She didn't make a sound. She just seemed to go limp.

'I stood up and grabbed the torch and shone it on her, and I could see the handle of the knife and the blood. Her hands had fallen away from it and she was not moving. Oh, God! It was awful.'

He stopped speaking. He held his face in his hands, rocking from side to side, living it all over again.

Drake said gently: 'What did you do then?'

He answered after a little while: 'I panicked. I just had to get away from there. I ran to the door and out of the barn.'

'But you went back, didn't you?'

'Yes. I don't know how far I ran. It seemed to be a long way. Then I stopped

236

and it occurred to me that perhaps she was not dead after all. I couldn't be sure if I didn't go back, so I had to go.'

'And she wasn't dead, was she?' Barling said.

Again Mark glanced at him in amazement. 'But of course she was.' He looked at Drake for an explanation. 'What does he mean?'

'There were two stab wounds in the body,' Drake said.

'But that's impossible. How could there be?'

'Why don't you tell us?' Barling said.

'I don't believe it.'

'You must believe it,' Drake said. 'It's fact. Do you still say you didn't stab her twice?'

'I didn't even stab her once. It was an accident.'

'If it was an accident why didn't you report it to the police?'

'I wanted to. I almost did. But I was afraid. I thought no one would believe me.'

'Smart lad,' Barling said. But Drake quelled him with a look.

'I'm afraid we shall have to take you in,' Drake said. He spoke regretfully. It was not something he liked doing. The boy seemed to be a decent sort, not a hooligan. He had probably never been in trouble before.

But it was necessary.

When they took her son away Mrs Ringer wept unrestrainedly. She was only thankful that Angela had not been there; she was having tea with a friend.

It had been a long day for Drake and Barling. Before going to their separate homes they had a last few words together.

'Do you think he did it, George?' the inspector asked.

'It's odds on,' Barling said.

'But why did he deny that second stabbing?'

'I'd say he's smart enough to see that it would put paid to his claim that it was an accident. You may stab somebody accidentally once, but not twice.'

'He seemed genuinely surprised to learn that there were two wounds.'

'Must have been pretending. If his tale was true he'd have noticed when he went back to see if the girl was dead.'

'Not necessarily. There was a lot of

blood and he was in a pretty confused state of mind. He might well have overlooked it.'

'So if he didn't do it, how did she come to be dead?'

'Well, try this for size. While he's out of the barn running like a hare somebody else goes in, sees the girl is still alive and gives her the *coup de grâce*. Then scarpers before he comes back.'

Barling thought about it. 'Crowther?'

'Could be.'

'Yes, I think it could. He's crafty enough. But I'd still say it's odds on the boy. Do you think she really meant to kill herself?'

'I very much doubt it. My guess is she was just putting on an act. Don't ask me why. Maybe simply for the hell of it, to scare him. She wasn't even going to have a baby; that was all hooey. The post-mortem revealed no evidence of pregnancy.'

'You think she made it up to put the bite on Crowther, and when it didn't work she took the knife as compensation?'

'Perhaps.'

'So why try it on the boy? She knew he hadn't a sou.'

'Maybe she even got herself believing it.

The human mind works in strange ways. One thing's certain: we'll never know now. She's saying nothing.'

'That's true. Good-night, Inspector.'

'Good-night, George.'

21 Touch-and-Go

When Maudie Maxted was found at the bottom of a disused gravel-pit with her skull fractured Howard Layton was inclined to think there was a hoodoo on The Merrymakers concert party.

Not that the death of Miss Maxted caused him anything like the amount of grief that the loss of his adored daughter had done; that was hardly to be expected. Maudie was just another member of the troupe; a likeable enough person but not one for whom he had any deep feeling. He would forget her in a few weeks, but Debbie would be in his heart for the rest of his life.

Jackie Vernon was the one most upset; which was only natural, bearing in mind the special kind of relationship that had existed between the two women. She it was who had first reported that Maudie had gone missing. And then a roadman came in with the news that he had discovered a body in the gravel-pit, and Sergeant Radford drove out there in his Hillman saloon with Constable Watson and confirmed that it was indeed Miss Maxted, whom both of them had seen around the village and on the stage of the Clover Hall.

Radford shook his head sadly. He did not think of hoodoos but he did think it curious that two of the entertainers should have come to a violent end within the space of a few days.

'There's lots of people I'd rather have seen go west than those two young people. What's things coming to in Braddlesham these days?'

Constable Watson, a stolid young man, had no opinion to advance on that subject, so he said nothing.

Miss Maxted was dressed only in a flimsy nightdress and a quilted dressing-gown, and she was lying at the foot of a sheer drop of some twenty feet. It was apparent that she had fallen from the grassy edge at the top, which was separated from the verge of the very minor road by a rough wooden fence. The two policemen had left the car on the road and had descended by way of a sloping track once used by lorries carrying away the gravel.

'You better stay here and see as nobody disturbs the body,' Radford said. 'I'll go back to the station and get things moving.'

Detective Inspector Drake had imagined that his work in Braddlesham was finished after the arrest of Mark Ringer, but the mysterious death of Maudie Maxted brought him back to the scene of his recent activities. For the fact was that a closer examination of the body than Sergeant Radford had given it revealed that the cause of Miss Maxted's death had not been the crushed skull consequent upon her fall into the old gravel-pit, and indeed it was probable that she had been dead some time before she arrived at that place. Marks on the neck clearly indicated strangulation, possibly by some form of ligature, and the implication was that she had been killed somewhere else and then transported to the pit and thrown into it.

So here again was Inspector Drake in Braddlesham, talking to people and looking for evidence; and it was natural that one of the first persons interviewed should be Jackie Vernon, who had been the dead woman's room-mate. Miss Vernon had been lying down and her face bore the evidence of recent tears, though she was no longer weeping when she opened the door of her room in answer to the inspector's discreet knock. He had come straight from the gravel-pit where he had acquainted himself with the physical features of the scene.

'May I come in, Miss Vernon? There are a few questions I should like to ask.'

'Of course, Inspector.'

She stood aside to let him pass, then closed the door. She was wearing slacks and a jumper, slippers on her feet. The black hair was not as smoothly brushed as usual; it was a trifle ruffled and there was about her a general impression of distress; which in the circumstances was only to be expected.

'You'll have to excuse the clutter,' she said. 'I just don't feel able to do anything.'

'I understand,' Drake said.

It was in fact an almost studied disorder; items of clothing thrown down just anywhere. There were two single beds, both of which appeared to have been slept in but not made up.

Miss Vernon removed a dress from one of the chairs and invited the inspector to sit down. She herself sat on one of the beds.

'I haven't let anybody come in here to do anything,' she said. 'I just couldn't.'

'Don't worry,' Drake said. 'It doesn't bother me. I believe it was you who discovered Miss Maxted's absence.'

'Yes. When I woke this morning I noticed at once that her bed was empty.'

'Was she in bed when you went to sleep?'

'Oh, yes.'

'Have you any idea when she got up?'

'No, I haven't. I sleep like a log. I didn't hear a thing.'

'Can you think of any reason why Miss Maxted should have got up in the night and left the room?'

Miss Vernon replied very promptly, as though she had been thinking about this question and had found an answer which satisfied her. 'She must have been sleep-walking again.'

'Sleep-walking! You mean she was a somnambulist?'

'Yes. It was something she was very sensitive about. I was the only one who knew; she made me promise not to tell anyone. Usually I would lock the door on the inside and keep the key under my pillow so that she wouldn't come to any harm, but last night I forgot. It was such a long time since she'd done anything of the sort and I thought she might have grown out of it. I blame myself for what happened.'

'What do you think happened?'

'But it's obvious, isn't it? She went downstairs, let herself out of the house and went for a walk. Some man must have seen her and killed her.'

'Why would he do that?'

'I don't know. There are perverts, aren't there? Homicidal maniacs. I suppose they prowl around looking for a likely victim. She must have been unlucky enough to meet one.'

'The body was found in a gravel-pit nearly a mile away. How did it get there?'

'Perhaps the killer was in a car; took her there and threw her in. It's a possibility, isn't it?'

'Oh, yes,' Drake said, 'it's certainly a possibility.' He stood up. 'I think perhaps

I'd better have a look at her things. Just routine.'

'Of course.'

There was not much. Like the late Miss Layton, Maudie Maxted had travelled around with all she owned in the world; which was very little. There was a battered suitcase, and in it were some odds and ends, including a sheaf of cuttings from provincial papers in which Miss Maxted had been mentioned. It was the nearest she had ever come to fame. There were no letters; no postcards even.

'Did she have any relations?' Drake asked.

'If she had, she never mentioned them to me. I think she'd cut herself off from anything of that sort. It was like the troupe had become all the family she needed.'

'I see.'

Drake picked up a silk stocking. 'This one of hers?'

'Yes.'

Drake held the stocking in both hands, stretching it in an absent-minded kind of way, apparently deep in thought. Miss Vernon watched him, saying nothing. He appeared to realize suddenly what he was doing and hung the stocking on the rail at the foot of one of the beds.

'Well, that's about all. I'll leave you now.'

He went downstairs and out into the yard at the back of the inn, where his car was parked. There was a glass-sided porch protecting the back door, and a young woman was just about to wheel a perambulator into it as Drake emerged. He recognized her as the landlord's daughter, a Mrs Clarice Smith, a plump friendly person to whom he had spoken on previous occasions. She was taking a holiday with her parents and occupied one of the spare rooms. In the perambulator was a baby girl, a few months old.

'You've been giving her an airing, I suppose,' Drake said.

'That's right. Getting quite a handful, she is.'

'She looks well,' Drake said. 'Going to be a pretty lady like her mum.'

Mrs Smith simpered. 'Go on with you, Inspector. You're trying to turn my head.'

The inspector put a finger into the pram and the baby grasped it. He made the sort of inane noises which are generally reckoned to be intelligible to the very young. The baby gurgled and dribbled.

'I suppose,' Drake said, 'you leave this pram in the porch at night?'

'Yes. It's the best place for it.'

Drake released his finger from the baby's grasp and looked thoughtfully at the wheels of the perambulator. Then he said: 'Well, this won't do. Mustn't hang about chatting to two charming young women. Work to do.'

He walked over to his car, got into it and drove out of the inn-yard. A few minutes later he was back at the gravel-pit. He got out of the car and began to examine the side of the road near where the body had gone over the brink of the pit. The road was tarred, but there was some sand that had collected near the verge. It was damp and there was an impression in it which could have been made by a narrow wheel. The daylight was fading, but Drake could see it clearly enough. There were also some scuff marks which might have been made by shoes.

Having completed his inspection Drake got into his car again, turned it and drove back to Braddlesham. He would have to have another talk with Miss Vernon, and this time it might be necessary to lean on her a bit.

As before he parked the car in the yard of the inn and went in by the back door. The perambulator was standing in the porch but there was no baby in it. Tom Simmonds met him as he was going in.

'You're soon back, Inspector,' Simmonds remarked.

'Yes. I want another word with Miss Vernon. Is she still in her room?'

'No, she ain't. You just missed her. She's gone.'

'Gone! Where?'

'London, I reckon. She got me to order Fred Pearce's taxi to take her to the station to catch the 6.28.'

'Damn it!' Drake said. 'She must have lost her nerve.' He glanced at his wristwatch. It was 6.22. He turned and ran out of the porch, heading for his car.

Simmonds watched him go, scratching his head in bewilderment.

Braddlesham Road Station was one-and-a-half miles out of the village. Drake hoped the train would be late, because otherwise it was going to be touch-and-go whether he got there before it carried Miss Vernon away on her journey to the metropolis. Not that that would be a complete disaster; a telephone call ought to ensure that she was picked up at Liverpool Street Station, but there was always the possibility that she might slip through. Better to catch her at this end.

There was a long straight section of road as you came towards the station, and across the flat ground on the right it was possible to see the train approaching if you were running things really close. As he came round the last bend Drake did in fact see the 6.28, the carriages all lighted up and visible through the gathering dusk. He put more pressure on the accelerator and raced the train, converging with it as they both approached the gates of the level-crossing.

He won the race by a narrow margin, brought the car to a skidding halt and jumped out. A small gate at the side of the crossing gave access to the platform and he was through and pounding up the ramp just as the engine came past the signal-box.

At first he thought the platform was deserted, but then he caught sight of a figure near the farther end, and as he ran towards it, keeping pace with the slowing train, he could see that it appeared to be a man wearing a trenchcoat and a wide-brimmed trilby hat. But he was not deceived and he gave a shout.

'Miss Vernon!'

She glanced in his direction and took fright at once. She had a suitcase with her but she abandoned it and started to run. But there was not much platform left for her, and suddenly she seemed to have a different idea. She stopped running and jumped down on to the track in front of the train.

'Oh, my God!' Drake muttered.

She nearly made it. The train was moving only very slowly now, and she must have reckoned that she could get across to the other side of the tracks while the inspector was baulked by the carriages. But she stumbled and the engine hit her.

Drake heard her scream.

22 Jealousy

Detective Inspector Drake went to the hospital accompanied by a detective constable whose job was to take things down. Drake had received a message from Miss

Vernon that she was prepared to talk to him, and he lost no time in responding to the invitation because anything that she had to say he would be very pleased to listen to.

He found her in a private room with a uniformed constable keeping watch outside. The constable was hardly necessary, since Miss Vernon, with a crushed leg and a broken arm and slight concussion, was in no condition to make a break for freedom. She looked very wan and sick, and it occurred to him that it might have been better for her if the train had killed her, because there really was not much future for her and there was a noose at the end of it.

'How are you feeling?' he asked.

She gave a wry smile. 'Would you believe me if I told you I was feeling on top of the world?'

He shook his head. 'No.'

'I feel like death,' she said.

He could think of nothing reassuring to say, so he said: 'You've decided to tell me everything, then?'

'Yes.'

'You know,' Drake said, 'I found it just a bit too hard to take that sleep-walking theory you put forward. I could see it was marginally possible. People do walk in their sleep. But it seemed too much of a coincidence that a sleep-walking Miss Maxted should have let herself out of the inn and run straight into a homicidal maniac on the prowl. In Braddlesham of all places.'

'Why not Braddlesham as well as anywhere else? Is it any better than the next place?'

Drake shrugged. He was not going to argue about that. 'At first,' he said, 'I didn't see how you could have transported the body to the gravel-pit. Then I saw the pram in the porch.'

'Ah!' she said. 'You don't miss much, do you?'

'I still don't understand why. I thought you and Miss Maxted were—'

'Lovers? Is that what you mean? You don't have to be shy about saying it. It happens, you know.'

'Yes, I do know. So again I ask, why?'

She sighed faintly. Her voice was weak, little more than a whisper, quite unlike the strong confident contralto he remembered.

'It has all to do with jealousy; the green-eyed monster.'

'Are you telling me you were jealous?'

'Oh, yes; horribly so.'

'But I don't understand. Who made you jealous?'

'Why, Debbie Layton, of course.'

Drake was bemused. He felt out of his depth.

She said: 'You still don't understand, do you?'

'No,' Drake said. 'You'll have to explain.' He glanced at the constable, who was scribbling on his pad. He wondered what that young man was making of it all. Perhaps he was not even attempting to make anything of it, just as long as he got it all down.

'I told you she was a minx, didn't I? I told you she liked to cause mischief in the company. That was why she got her claws into Maudie; because she knew it would upset me. It was sheer spite; I don't think she cared two pins for Maudie really; she wasn't inclined that way. It was all a pretence, but Maudie fell for it, went overboard for her. I tried to talk her out of it, tried to make her see reason; but it was no use.'

'I see,' Drake said. He was beginning to see quite a lot now; and Hugh Crowther was being pushed more and more out of the reckoning. 'Miss Maxted wasn't your first victim, was she?'

Miss Vernon gave a slightly malicious grin, revealing her strong white teeth. 'Now you're being smart, Inspector.'

'Are you going to tell me how it happened?'

'Of course. Why else would I have invited you here? Where do you want me to start?'

'How about the beginning?'

'Oh, no, that's far too long ago; lost in the mists of time. I'll start where Debbie walked out of the Queen's Head that Sunday evening.'

'You saw her go?'

'Yes. She was coming out of her room in her mac, and I knew she had to be going out. So I nipped back into my room, put on a coat and followed her.'

'Why?'

'I wanted to have it out with her. I thought maybe if I got her alone I could persuade her to break it off with Maudie. I thought I might even threaten to tell her father what was going on, though of course he would never have believed it and she would have sworn blind it was all lies.'

'So,' Drake said, 'you followed her just to reason with her? Nothing else?'

Jackie Vernon gave a low mocking laugh. 'Oh, I know what you're getting at. But you're wrong. It wasn't in my mind at all. I didn't even have a weapon.'

'True. Maybe it was the devil who provided that. Did you have any difficulty in keeping her in sight?'

'None at all. There was enough moonlight. And she never once looked back to see if anyone was following.'

'Why didn't you overtake her if all you wanted was a private talk?'

'I thought about it, but then curiosity got the better of me. I wanted to discover where she was going. I felt sure she wasn't just walking for the pleasure of it.'

'And so you found she was going to Longmere Hall?'

'Yes. It surprised me. I had no idea she knew Mr Crowther. I followed her up the drive and hid behind a shrub when she got to the house. I saw a maid come to the door and let her in.'

'But you didn't go away even then?'

'No. I waited and waited. It was cold and I was shivering, but I refused to go. Then suddenly the door opened and she came running out. She ran down the drive and I followed, though it was all I could do to keep up with her at first. Then she slowed down to a walk and it was easier. We were getting near the village then, and I had just decided to catch up and have it out with her when she disappeared. I couldn't think where she had gone, but then I came to a gateway in the hedge and I could see a glimmer of light coming from that old barn and I guessed that was where she'd gone.'

She paused, and Drake saw that her eyes were closed, as though she had suddenly fallen asleep. But it was only a moment of weakness or pain, and then she opened the eyes again and continued speaking.

'I went up to the barn door, and there was a chink which made it possible to see inside. And there they were.'

'They?'

'Her and the boy.'

'You mean Mark Ringer?'

'I didn't know who he was then. I do now, of course.'

'What were they doing?'

'Just talking. Though I couldn't hear what they were saying. Then suddenly she hauled a knife out of her coat pocket and held it with the point towards her as if she meant to kill herself. He made a grab at her; I think he was trying to stop her; but she fell over backwards and he fell on top of her. His weight must have pushed the knife into her. He got up at once, but she was still lying on a heap of hay and not moving.'

'What did he do then?'

'He picked up the torch that was on the floor and shone it on her. Then he gave a sort of sobbing cry and ran out of the barn. I just had time to get out of the way and he didn't even see me; he just kept on running.'

'So then?'

'Then I went into the barn. I had a small pocket-torch with me, and I shone it on Debbie and could see she wasn't dead. She must have fainted when the knife went in, but she was coming round and seemed to be trying to say something. It made me mad. I kept thinking why couldn't she be dead? It would have solved my problem. It really burned me up. I got so that I just couldn't leave it like that; I was so full of anger and hate and everything. So I put the torch down and gripped the knife with both hands and pulled it out of her and drove it in again as hard as I could.'

'Then you wiped the handle to remove your fingerprints?'

'I didn't have to. I was wearing gloves.'

'Ah!' And Mark Ringer had not touched the knife, so if there had been any prints they would have been the victim's. And maybe they had been obliterated by Miss Vernon's gloves.

'I suppose you left the barn then?'

'Yes.'

'Did you see Mark Ringer come back?'

'Yes. He went past me like a madman. I was not five yards away from him and he didn't see me. I didn't hang around then. I went straight back to the Queen's Head and to my room.'

'Was Miss Maxted there?'

'No. She was down in the bar, drinking, with Dickie Wilson.'

'So she was friendly with him?'

'Not really. I suppose they were both feeling a bit down because of the cancellation of the Sawborough run.'

'Drowning their sorrows?'

'That's about it.'

'So what did you do when you'd got to your room?'

'I stayed there for a time, pulling myself

together. I was in a very excited state; not remorseful, not a bit of that, but excited. I took off my gloves and coat and examined them carefully. There was some blood on the gloves but not a sign of any on the coat. So I hung the coat in the wardrobe and put the gloves in an empty chocolate box and got rid of them the next day.'

'How did you do that?'

'I got up early, went down to the river and dropped the box over the parapet of the bridge. It just floated away on the current. I expect it sank later.'

'Clever,' Drake said.

'Wasn't it! Well, after I'd put the gloves in the chocolate box and stowed it away in my suitcase for the time being I changed my shoes, which were a bit muddy, and went down to the bar and joined Maudie and Dickie. Maudie asked where I'd been and I said for a walk. She gave me an old-fashioned look but said nothing. "Well, good for you," Dickie said. "Keeping yourself fit for when we start working again." And then he added gloomily: "If we ever do".

'The Drings and Howard and Gloria Layton were also in the bar, killing time before going to bed; but of course there was no sign of Debbie. Maudie said she wondered where she was, and Dickie said he guessed she was up to no good wherever she was. But he didn't say it loud enough for the Laytons to hear. "One day," he said, "that girl is going to get herself into real trouble. You mark my words." Which was pretty perceptive of him when you come to think about it.'

'Yes, it was,' Drake said. 'But none of this explains why you killed Miss Maxted.'

'I'm coming to that. It was all because of the way she took on over the death of Debbie. She kept saying how much she missed her and sighing like a love-sick girl and all that. It really got on my nerves. It was so stupid. Debbie had never had any real feeling for her, and yet here she was acting in this ridiculous way. It was as we were getting ready to go to bed that night when it finally blew up. She was going on and on, and I suppose I just went crazy. I told her I was the one who killed Debbie and I was glad I did it because she was nothing but a little good-for-nothing bitch who was best out of the way.'

'How did she take that?' Drake asked.

'She wouldn't believe it at first. She said I was making it up. So I told her just

261

how it happened and how it was what I was doing when I was out walking that Sunday evening. Finally it seemed to sink in, but she didn't go wild or anything like I thought she might. Instead, she just stared at me and said very quietly: "I shall tell the police. You won't get away with this."

'It was then it dawned on me what a mistake I'd made, and I knew there was only one thing to do. I had to kill her. In a way you might say she'd brought it on herself by all that moaning. Or if you go back a bit further it was Debbie's fault for playing around with her.'

It amazed Drake that she could excuse herself like this. She had killed two people and was blaming them for it. It was a curious shifting of responsibility, but it was apparent that she had genuinely convinced herself that she had not been at fault but had simply been the victim of circumstance.

'You used a stocking, of course? For the ligature.'

She gave a faint smile. 'I knew that was what you were thinking when you picked that one up and stretched it between your hands. I could see your mind working, and I knew then I had to get away.'

'So I was right?'

'No; you were wrong. Would a silk stocking have been strong enough? I don't really know. But actually it was the cord from my dressing-gown.'

Drake nodded. 'Yes, that would do the job.'

'It was not particularly difficult,' Miss Vernon said. 'I don't think she had the least suspicion of what I was about to do. She was standing there in her nightdress, and I moved suddenly round behind her and gave her a push which sent her face down on to the bed. I put a knee on her back and slipped the cord round her neck and twisted it tight. She made choking noises and struggled a bit, but I was too strong for her and after a while she stopped struggling and was dead.'

Just like that, Drake thought. No emotion showing. Cool as could be. Pausing for breath.

The young constable was looking at her now, fascinated. He had probably never come across anyone quite like Jackie Vernon. Perhaps there was no one like her.

'And then?' Drake said.

'Then I put the dressing-gown on her

and got myself dressed and waited. It was already getting on for midnight, and I gave it another hour or so. I opened the door and there wasn't a sound in the place; everybody was asleep. I picked her up. She was just a little wisp of a thing, and like I said, I'm strong. I carried her out of the room and shut the door. There was no light on anywhere and it was pitch-dark, but I knew where the stairs were, and I carried her down and out into the back porch where I knew the landlord's daughter kept her pram. I lifted Maudie into it and her legs were sticking out at the front, but there was nothing I could do about that. So then I got the pram out on to the road and pushed it up to the old gravel-pit and dropped her in.'

'You knew it was there?'

'Well, no. I was just going to dump her somewhere, anywhere, in a wood or something. But when I got there it seemed just the place. I could see the fence in the moonlight, and I took a look and there was the pit on the other side.'

'And then you pushed the pram back to the Queen's Head and went to bed?'

'Yes.'

'You didn't meet anyone on the road?

No cars or anything?'

'No. At that time of night in the country I don't suppose many people are about. It's not like London.'

The question had no bearing on the matter, but Drake felt compelled to ask it.

'Did you sleep well?'

'Oddly enough,' she said, 'it was like I told you. I slept like a log.'

Yes, Drake thought, she would. She would probably sleep like a log the night before they hanged her.

23 A Long Time Ago

It was the end of the road for The Merrymakers. Perhaps, Howard Layton reflected, they had been dead already; perhaps the two murders just put the last nails in the coffin. It was the end of his stage career also. Years later he still used to talk of it to anyone who would listen; telling them about the wonderful daughter who would have made a name for herself if she had not met an untimely death at the hands of a wicked woman.

He was running a small tobacconist's shop at that time, having been helped to take it with a loan from a sympathetic relative. The living quarters behind the shop were filled with pictures of Deborah, which he would show to people time and again.

'She was so talented, you know. She would have been a hit on the London stage for certain. Then films, Elstree, Hollywood...'

As time went by he seemed to find it more and more difficult to separate fact from fiction. Hollywood became not just an unfulfilled dream but a reality. She was actually out there making films, maybe with Fred Astaire. She had become 'My daughter Deborah, the film star, you know. She doesn't come home much these days; far too busy. But one day...'

The Drings never appeared on the stage again. They had put a little money away and they opened a dancing school which operated under the rather classy title of The Dring Academy of Terpsichore. Amazingly, it prospered, and they were soon earning far more by teaching other people to dance than they had ever made doing all the hard work themselves with The Merrymakers concert party.

Sometimes they would become reminiscent about old times, and Dorothy would say: 'Do you remember that day when Dickie Wilson got drunk and insulted me, and you punched him in the eye and knocked him down?'

'Do I not?' Desmond would say. 'I wonder what he's doing now? On his beam-ends, I shouldn't wonder.'

But in fact Dickie Wilson was far from that, though he had never made it to the top. He was spotted in a pantomime in Leeds by the widow of a millionaire financier. She snapped him up like a blackbird snapping up a tasty worm and they were married within the month.

She was no chicken and had never had any claims to beauty, but he was perfectly happy. She was able to provide him with everything he had ever asked of life: money.

After his release from the detention centre where he had been held with other young offenders Mark Ringer went back to Braddlesham and the correspondence course. But his heart was not in the work and it all came to nothing. Years of frustration were to follow: trying for one job after another without success, helping in the shop and hating it, while the war clouds gathered over Europe and diplomats scurried hither and thither like frightened ants. Where was it all leading?

Oddly enough, it was the war that was to release him from his misery. He was called up to serve his country and found himself pitchforked into the Royal Navy. His early dream had been of a seafaring life, and now the dream had come true in a completely unexpected way. Not that the role of an able-bodied seaman on board a viciously rolling corvette escorting a convoy in the North Atlantic was quite what he had envisaged in those far off days, but you had to take things as they came. At least when ashore he could swagger with the best and feel a sense of pride in his bell-bottomed trousers and sailor's cap.

And he was a hero now, in the eyes of his family if in no one else's. Even Angela, who had joined the Auxiliary Territorial Service, wrote him long letters full of love and admiration.

A hero! Him!

What, he wondered, would Debbie have said to that? She would have laughed no doubt. Anyway, it did not pain him to think of her now. That wound had healed and she was just an incident in the past. Once he had imagined he could not live without her; now he knew that he could.

Hugh Crowther enlisted in the army on the outbreak of war and was soon given a commission. He volunteered for one of the crazier special units, rose to the rank of captain and won the Military Cross. He was idolized by his men, who would have followed him anywhere. He was wounded twice and told everyone afterwards that the years of combat were the best of his life. He had enjoyed every minute of it.

One evening during his army service he was persuaded to go to a show given by the Entertainments National Service Association. It lived up to the reputation of ENSA: Every Night Something Awful. In a way it reminded him of that troupe which used to come ot Braddlesham. What was the name of it? The Merrymakers, wasn't it? And there was that girl who got herself killed with his paper-knife of all things. Remembered her name now: Debbie. Pretty kid.

What a long time ago! What a hell of a long time ago!

The publishers hope that this book has given you enjoyable reading. Large Print Books are especially designed to be as easy to see and hold as possible. If you wish a complete list of our books, please ask at your local library or write directly to: Dales Large Print Books, Long Preston, North Yorkshire, BD23 4ND, England.

This Large Print Book for the Partially sighted, who cannot read normal print, is published under the auspices of

THE ULVERSCROFT FOUNDATION